REVERIE

The incredibly talented Joseph John Sanchez III designed the perfect cover art for this book. Please go buy his art at www.joejohnart.com.

Cameron Curtis edited the mess I handed him and has always believed in me and encouraged me.

Dedication:

This book is a love letter to Wenatchee, Washington. I am forever grateful to this beautiful valley for her protection and inspiration and to her people for their support and wisdom.

Acknowledgements:

My husband, Steve Robey, thank you for loving me in ways I never thought possible. I couldn't have done this without you. My handsome, loud, strong sons: thank you everything you are and will be.

And last but never least - my amazing community of friends: I am so lucky to have you all.

Chapter 1:

I shared the last 30 seconds of my walk into the grocery store with an older woman this afternoon. I sensed movement and life slightly behind me and glanced. I tossed her a smile and she returned it.

I pulled out a cart for myself and offered to do the same for her. She politely told me she likes the little black ones and I dreamed of the day where I could fit all my groceries in the same. I gallantly pulled her preferred cart from the corral for her and we parted ways. I studied her petite frame as she bee-lined for the deli cheese island and my weird brain did the thing it does and I imagined the life this woman lived to get here today.

She was thin, maybe 5'0". I'm bad at guessing ages, but her gait and hair color make me think she was a nicely preserved late 60s. Dressed simply but with a precision, her periwinkle button-up was ironed with expertly rolled sleeves. I name her Janice.

Janice Marie Stephenson, the oldest and ultimately only daughter of Bothell's John and Mary-Margaret Stephenson. When Janice was 4-years-old, she helped her mother pin-set her hair and noticed a growing stomach. Her mother excitedly told her she was going to be a big sister. Unfortunately, after the family had brought the crib in from the garage and her mother had sewed a whole layette set, the baby never came. The family rarely discussed the loss, but Janice more so missed her mother's gay piano playing the hour before bedtime than her potential sibling.

She was an average student with perfect penmanship, voted 'shyest' by her high school class. Janice wasn't shy to those who knew her best, she's just a bit quiet and reserved. Her friend group was small but close. In fact, one of those high school girls was the reason she was at the market today, but we'll get to that. She was the fastest in her typewriting class and recruited before she graduated for the stenographer's program. Three months of training later, she was gainfully employed by King County, mostly working in the municipal court recording the quibbles over traffic infractions. She was also being courted by an ambitious, if a bit boring, assistant district attorney (who'd already named their future children, much to Janice's dissatisfaction). They ate lunch together every day at the same table in the courthouse deli, where the man ate his ham and swiss, untoasted, and never noticed her new blouse or broach.

Janice accepted her likely fate, knowing a proposal was on the horizon. He'd asked her ring size and took her father out for a drink. America's youth was experiencing its Summer of Love, but Janice was Episcopalian. She knew her ADA was the benign bet and she'd be as happy as she ever could have hoped to be. This was until Ralph Roberts ran into her courtroom, late and disheveled. She shook her head at his untucked shirt and waited for the judge to admonish him. Ralph was there to argue a speeding ticket he'd received, a hefty fine of $50 for 25 miles over the limit. Janice watched in awe as the man masterfully began orating the circumstances that found him in that courthouse. Twice she had to reset her perfectly trained hands, as she was losing focus on her only job. Ralph was a car salesman and by the end of his speech had convinced the judge the speeding was entirely necessary to do his job and maybe even sold the older man on the newest model of Skylark.

He'd certainly sold himself to Janice.

A week later, after an uncomfortable conversation with a certain attorney, Janice found herself at the Buick dealership looking for a test drive. It was perhaps the gutsiest thing she'd ever done in her life, but even now, 50 years later, she'd have zero regrets. The test drive led to meeting for a drink and two weeks later the pair wed in the glow of the neon lights of Las Vegas. Janice wore white pedal-pushers and two strangers playing craps were their witnesses. It was the first of thousands of adventures they would share. Ralph was persuasive, sure, but also brilliant. He invested in a Toyota Dealership right before the 70s gas crisis and made a fortune on economic imports.

They'd discussed children once, but loved each other too much to share. Sure, people asked questions but it never bothered them. They lived downtown and never once used their kitchen. They worked hard but traveled often. Janice would show Ralph pictures from her beloved National Geographic magazine and he'd make the trip happen. The two saw the Buddhas of Bamiyan, walked the Great Wall, swam with dolphins, ate fresh Mexican tamales after exploring ancient ruins, and, of course, kissed in Paris. In 2013, Ralph sold their condo and the dealership and they decided to spend the rest of their 3rd act as RV people - American nomads. They only made it through 4 states when Ralph's giant heart surrendered and widowed a devastated Janice.

Her best friend from high school wrote to her through that insipid facebook. She was also recently widowed and living in Wenatchee. The women shared feelings of helplessness and incurable loss, eventually deciding to share living space as well. Janice sold the RV and took up a North Central Washington residency. The two women have a glorious view and a pathetic backyard garden. They laugh a lot and the nice neighbor guy showed them how to use Netflix. It's Janice's turn to 'make' dinner which means a trip to Safeway for some good cheese, cured meats, and a bottle of wine or two. Probably two.

I feel a hand on my shoulder, "Ma'am, are you okay?"

Oh, no. I've done it again. I come to my senses and realize I've been blocking most of the aisle. I shake out of my daydream and wonder how long I've been standing here. I tell the young woman I am fine and quickly finish my shopping.

***

I've been like this for as long as I can remember. I recall being a small child and fascinated by people and their stories. My mother would have to silence me around strangers, asking them the unaskable: "Why are you a cashier?" "Why did you have kids?" "How did you get so fat?" I know now exactly how the last one happens, as I gaze down at my mom-paunch. I throw the meatloaf into the stove and start peeling the potatoes. I know this is all in vain, my husband will have eaten at work and my sons will pick at the meal and only eat a few bites.

Hell, I don't even like meatloaf. But it was all I could think to cook.

***

The next morning, I carefully make myself a sandwich with slices of the cold meatloaf and glide mayonnaise over white bread. This is why I make meatloaf; I think. I love the sandwiches after. I glance out my kitchen window to my lovely, suburban street. Alice across the way is already kneeling carefully at her front flower bed, pulling the dastardly weeds from their roots and tossing them into a pile at her side.

I know almost nothing about the woman. I don't think she

works, at least not traditionally. She spends a great deal of time on her immaculate garden and seems too young to be a retiree. She lives alone and hasn't been interested in being all that social with me. I guess I could reach out more, but I'm a busy working mom of two. She lived there when we moved in a decade ago and I only know her name and that her sister visits every Christmas.

I wonder if she's a novelist maybe: Wenatchee's own Agatha Christie. Maybe she gardens all day and writes at night with a glass of wine. A spinster-in-training, too young to hold the official title. Maybe she's an heiress who threw away big city life to live anonymously in the mountainous valley. Oh, maybe she's in witness protection.

She was young when she met Vinny. Her name was Jessi and at 19, she was full of dreams to make it as a Vegas showgirl. Vinny had money and connections, took her to all the major events and concerts - box seats, high roller suites, bottle service. VIP Vinny. He purchased her designer clothing and big flashy jewelry. He surprised her with a luxury apartment, all her own. She'd been living in a one-bedroom dumpster-fire with three roommates, all dancers. She learned a few months into the relationship she was a 'kept woman', never to be the wife, never to ask for more than a few hours of his time. She settled for the arrangement, not knowing much about his criminal life or family.

Vinny was unpredictable. The first time he hit her, she was so surprised it took her well into the next day to process the abuse. The slap came out of nowhere when she expressed that she didn't want sushi for dinner, as she didn't really like it. The affection after the slap was so fast and so grand it overpowered everything else. She'd never felt his love and care in that way. Over time the slaps became punches and the aftermath grew less gracious. In a year, she found herself trapped, regular abuse with a gorgeous view of The Strip.

Vinny was spiraling. He installed a large safe in the apartment and threatened her viciously to never, ever look inside or show it to anyone. Not that she was allowed guests in her own home. She started saving small amounts of cash in the lining of her favorite jacket. She had a dream to walk away one day and start over. She started quietly pawning older pieces of jewelry he'd given her. She started noticing patterns with the safe. She knew on days he'd secretly place plain, brown paper bags in the vault, Vinny would be in high spirits and have lots of cash for the casino that night. She had guessed drugs or maybe some sort of underground gambling. Vinny was 'family', Vegas' quiet little mafia, but not super high up, as far as she could tell.

Some nights, Vinny would use her apartment for a card game. She could tell who the big boss was on those nights. She would instinctively serve his drinks first and Vinny approved.

Some nights, Vinny would inquire about the girl's past. On those quiet nights he was back to the adoring man in love from the beginning of their time together. She told him of her days as a shy, skinny ballerina in Trenton, New Jersey. How the kids teased her for knobby knees and would sing Jessi's Girl at her. She would softly stroke his hair and talk about her mom and dad, Carol and Ralphie. She felt almost safe on those sweet nights.

One day, after a decidedly not-safe night, she saw her chance. Vinny stood at the open safe with a good drunk-on. She had the silencer screwed on to the small handgun he'd given her 'just in case' and popped two the back of his head without hesitation. She looked into the paper bags and saw more than her coat lining could dare to ever hold. She packed it into a small suitcase with a few pieces of jewelry and some clothes. She had the door-man call her a cab to the airport.

She took a bus from the airport to Reno and purchased a junker car with cash. She drove it to Idaho, where she reunited with her sister and mother. You see, she was smarter than Vinny could have guessed. The 'family' would be looking for the wrong girl in the wrong part of the country: she'd made everything up.

She settled on Wenatchee as her forever home after some research into ballet studios seeking instructors. She purchased her home with a surprising cash down and worked for a few years until her knees couldn't handle it. She lives peacefully on Maiden Lane, never looking over her shoulder in fear and happy to be alone.

Oh, crap, I'm late for work.

***

As always, work is a bit boring. I've worked at Ripkin Insurance since I was 20. My father got me the job; I answer the phone and process the paperwork for the agents. My father was in Kiwanis with Frank Ripkin Sr. I've recently celebrated 15 years with the agency and they got me a cake and lovely card. I overheard one of the younger agents whispering to another that she couldn't believe I'd stayed at my position so long. She postulated that I certainly should have ambition to be an agent or work my way up to something, anything.

I suppose it's a bit monotonous, but I like the hours and like the consistency. I'm able to be a mom, which I've always put before my career. My husband makes more than enough to pay the bills, but I like contributing. Also, there's excellent people watching from my desk in the front office in Wenatchee's bustling downtown. Just now I look up and see a man on a bicycle, in a skin-tight racing outfit, as if the Tour de France was cruising Central Washington. Why would he be in such a get-up at 9:00AM on a weekday?

Is he in training? He looks a bit too old to be competitive. I mean, he's in great shape, but there's silver hair peeking through the back of his helmet and lines on his face. I peg him to be one of those Iron Men, training for a rigorous marathon of biking, kayaking, and running. He takes two mornings of the week to devote to training for each, rotating cycling on Mondays and Thursdays, running is for Tuesdays and Fridays, and he kayaks on Wednesdays and Saturdays. Sundays he rests, only light weight training. He rolls into work a bit later, around 10, but stays late to get everything done.

Or has a flexible schedule to allow him his training. Maybe he's in advertising or music production. A rarity for our small town, but not unheard of.

After his divorce, Alex, yes definitely an Alex, decided to win by getting as fit as humanly possible. That will show Kim, his ex. And her new boyfriend Tony. Fucking Tony, as he calls him, with his stupid ponytail and jacked up ancient Jeep. Fucking Tony and Kim, in the house he built, living on a third of his paycheck. Alex hates Kim and Fucking Tony with a vitriol that concerns his friends. He uses the hatred to fuel his workouts, an emotional Cliff Bar.

"Nan? Nan. Nancy!" I see movement to my right. An agent named Todd is trying to get my attention. I look over to him. He asked me to make 3 copies of the contract in his hand. I smile as I take the papers, walk two feet over and make his copies. I can't imagine having the gall to ask someone to do this task for me. He was actually closer to the machine than I was.

I hand them to him, delightfully warm from the copier. He chuckles and says, "Wow, you were in your own little world there, weren't you?"

I give him a thin-lipped half smile. "Thank God you were around to rope me back in."

I sit back down but Alex, his fanny-pack, and his anger are long gone.

***

I'm trying to explain how our fax system works to a senior agent, and how I've already sent his anticipated fax in a PDF to his email. He was having none of it and insisted I print it out for him instead. I make a silent prayer to myself that I won't be this technologically inept in my silver years, but am reminded that my kid had to set up my Spotify for me.

I glance out my beloved window and see a young couple, clearly in the depths of early love. She gayly holds his hand and rests her head against his shoulder, enraptured by his every word. I can't remember the last time I held my husband's hand. I start to wonder about this couple, where they're off to today, but catch myself and focus on work. Inspiration strikes and I pick up my phone and call my husband's cell.

He doesn't answer. That's to be expected; he's probably with a patient. My husband owns a chiropractic clinic, thrice voted Wenatchee's Best by our local paper. I call his receptionist, Marcy, on her direct line. She answers promptly and informs me, yes, Daniel is with a patient but will call me back as soon as he can.

Marcy is such a lovely woman. I'd offered to be Daniel's receptionist back when he opened the practice but we both agreed maybe it would be best for our marriage if we didn't spend both night and day together. He's so popular and busy now, I wonder if I should offer it again. I'd hate to displace Marcy, though. I enjoy visiting with her when I stop by. I wonder if she'd be interested in a trade: would she be happy at Ripkin Insurance? Am I happy?

I'm not unhappy. Like I said, I like my hours. My sons have constant after school activities and I'm either taxiing or making snacks or sewing patches most afternoons. I truly adore Frank Sr., but he's rarely in the office anymore. Frank Jr., or Frankie as he still insists on being called despite nearing 60-years-old, is a certified jerk. I hate the way he speaks to us, especially me. On the rare occasion I make a mistake, he's so fast to call me stupid or flakey. Yeah, I may inwardly wander from time to time, but I'm not stupid. I'm mentally squishing Frank Jr's tiny head when my husband calls me back.

"Hey babe." I'm thrilled for the distraction, and trying to remember how it felt when we were in new love.

"What's wrong?" He asks with no emotion. I guess I don't randomly call him much these days.

"How busy is your day?" I ask. "I was thinking maybe we could meet up for lunch or something."

"Oh." He says simply. He then audibly exhales. "Today is stacked up. I doubt I'll have much time to eat, I'm just gonna order a salad or something." He is such a healthy eater, I'm so proud of him. "I'll be late again too." He adds.

"Oh, ok. Patty-Cake has a game tonight, remember?" Our younger son, Patrick, is a promising forward. The practice and game schedule can be exhausting, but our sons being active in sports is super important to Daniel. Danny was a bit geeky and withdrawn when he was young, he wants our sons to understand teamwork and the value of physical activity.

"Right, right, you're still doing that. Ok, love, I have a patient, see you later." He hangs up before I get the chance to say any kind of salutation. My husband has never been one for sentiment anyway.

I look down at my belly. Maybe I should toss the meatloaf sandwich and get a salad too. Or start training for an Iron Man or something.

***

The orange slices perfectly arranged in my largest Tupperware, check. Sports drinks and water bottles covered in ice in our specified game cooler, check. It only took a few minutes to prepare the slices, but I'm annoyed. I almost always bring snacks for the team. One time, just once, I brought apple slices instead of orange and Coach lost it. I would be so bored of them.

That coach is a tough nut to crack. Patty, now 12-years-old, is on two teams. His regular school team is in the fall, but he's also in a competitive youth soccer league that plays in the summer. This is our last game for our summer season, as school started a couple weeks ago. We've known the coach, who insists even parents call him Coach Davis, for three years now and I have trouble with how hard he is on the kids. Daniel insists it's for their own good, but I wince at his yelling at least once a game.

I don't think he grew up here. He's about my age and if he was a local, I would have some vague connection to him. Wenatchee is a small town. Sometimes when he's yelling at the kids, I detect an almost Bostonian accent. I bet he's from that area.

He's an asshole so his name is obviously like Kent or Jarod. Kent. Kent Davis from a wealthy suburb of Boston, born to Suzanne and George Davis: their eldest and only son. His two little sisters would barely register to George, however. He had the son he always wanted to shape and mold into the next great American quarterback. Little Kent was never photographed without a football in his hand. His father, a failed B-string cornerback for UMass, is an assistant coach for a university that you never directly say, only hint to. A university where tuition is the same price as a brand-new car every semester.

George put little Kent in Pop Warner and had him on a daily calisthenics and cardio routine by the age of six. Kent also secretly took ballet and gymnastics to improve his agility, but George took him to classes nearly an hour away, lest anyone see his son in tights. Kent was a little delayed in academics and speech, but a natural athlete. Kent also had a secret he would never, ever say out loud to another human.

He loves marbles.

He loves everything about them. He loves the fabrication, the grace and beauty of the shiny spheres, the gameplay (India rules, obviously, the British style is nonsense). Kent's obsession with marbles was suppressed at every opportunity by his father. He learned quickly to keep it private. His mother indulged it, secretly taking the boy to the toy stores and antique stores to add to his collection. He had giant ones and tiny ones, mass-produced and hand made. He begged his mother to take him to a glass maker someday so he could watch how they're made.

When Kent was 10-years-old, his team lost the division championship for his youth league, partially due to Kent underestimating a crucial pass and basically throwing the ball into the hands of the opposition. George was furious and to teach his son a lesson, threw his large mason jar of marbles in the garbage. Kent knew better than to cry, but he ran to his room in despair. His mother would later retrieve the jar from the garbage and offer to hide his collection from George, but it was too late for Kent. The rift had begun. Kent refused to play football ever again. His father signed him up and drove him to practices and games, but Kent remained steadfastly on the bench. Eventually, the man gave up.

In high school, Kent signed himself up for the soccer team. He was a natural athlete and learned the sport easily, making varsity as a freshman. He would earn a scholarship to University of Washington, one of the biggest schools for the sport. His father never attended one game. The two speak maybe five words to each other a year. Kent fell in love with a hippy chick on the girl's team and they married after sophomore year. She happily made centerpieces filled with marbles for the reception.

Kent blew out his knee his senior year, but was happy to follow the family tradition of coaching. His wife wanted to come home to Wenatchee to open a yoga studio and he coaches this summer competitive league and at the community college. They divorced years ago, but he stayed in the Valley to co-parent their daughter, a natural athlete who genuinely loves soccer.

"Mom?!" Patrick is getting my attention.

"Hey, buddy, you ready?" I ask happily.

"Yeah, I have been waiting in the van. You're so weird sometimes." I shrug. He isn't wrong.

Chapter 2:

As he handed my change back, the cashier looked away from my smiling face. Perhaps afraid to catch my optimism, perhaps turned off by women of a certain size or age. I wasn't hurt, it didn't matter, but his action sent my mind into one of its fits and I began to wonder who this cashier was and what led to this moment.

His thick, glorious, enviable hair was much longer than most men wear it, almost to his collar. He seems a little old for trying to grow it long, most men try that in their teens and early twenties. The cashier had crow's feet, a rounded paunch, and enough gray hair to count as a percentage. On looks alone, I'd put him at 35. That means his name is Matthew, Michael, or Christopher. He's a Christopher, I see it now. He hates when you call him Chris.

Christopher made no plans for college because he was certain he'd never see adulthood. When he was four-years-old, his mother lost him briefly in a department store and, teamed with his father, drowned poor little Christopher with the certain knowledge that he would someday be abducted. It wasn't a fear; it was an inevitability. Christopher would lethargically shrug when asked his occupational aspirations, for it would never be a possibility. He was destined to disappear into the back of some kid-toucher's van, never seen or heard from again. He'd played the scenario in his head so many times it no longer scared him. He was grateful when it got delayed long enough to allow him to attend his friend's 10th birthday party, where he got to eat junk food and watch an R-Rated movie (with boobies!).

He struggled in high school because he never had to try at anything and had no muscle for it. He barely graduated, only by threats of bodily harm by his father, and made a half-hearted attempt at junior college. He didn't graduate, but he did meet a friend that changed his life. The friend, let's call him Brandon, introduced Christopher to on-line gaming. Christopher's academics didn't last a semester against World of Warcraft.

Ever since, he's worked jobs that pay him just enough to cover his bills so he can spend at least 30 hours a week with his real passion. He barely puts effort into his work, knowing they'll keep him around as long as he doesn't goof up too badly. He knows people judge what he does; his family thinks it's an addiction. He couldn't care less. He's happy. He's elated to be alive and not a long-forgotten photo on a milk carton, living in a world of his choice and his creation.

"Did you need something else?" Christopher asks impatiently.

"Oh! Sorry! Bit slow today. Guess I really need this!" I pointed to the canned iced coffee that was half of my breakfast. The other half consists of a roll of chocolate covered mini-donuts. They're garbage, but I need a little boost. He couldn't care less and stares at me until I leave.

***

I'm taking the day off from work. I don't do this often, but the office will survive without me. I had too many time-sensitive errands stacking up so I scheduled them all for today to knock them out. First is an oil change, then I will check my older son, DJ (Daniel Junior) out of school for his sports physical and checkup. His 16th birthday is coming up and I will let him drive us on his learner's permit, getting him as much practice as possible before his big test.

I absolutely cannot believe my baby; my little baby boy is almost 16. I remember it so clearly, his bright gray eyes and the fat rolls on his legs. I was 19 when I had him, a bit on the young side, but oh, so ready to be a mom.

I love this little alignment shop/oil change place on the east side. There's never a wait and the owner is this charismatic Russian guy who calls everyone by the celebrity he thinks they look like. He calls me Tina Fey; I don't see it but I think it's sweet and hilarious.

"Hey Tina Fey, you want for tranny flush too?" He is a born salesman.

"No, just the oil change, please." I smile. It's worth the extra ten minutes to come to this place. I take a seat in the tiny waiting area. They've cleverly retrofitted three race car seats into their lobby chairs. The floor is checkerboarded and every accessory is chrome or other minutia of racing life. Not my style, at all, but fun.

An older man is already seated. He acknowledges me with a nod and I return it. I imagine his name is Bill. Well, actually William Allen Jacobson. He's a real local, lived in Wenatchee his whole life, minus his obligatory four years in the Navy. His high school sweetie, Sandra, waited for him and they wed one week after he returned from Korea. He says vaguely racist things about his time there, but remained unharmed as he was in communications.

The love of amateur band radio was born during his time overseas. For a living, Bill sold farm equipment for orchardists, but on his own time - Bill was on the air. After he and Sandra saved the customary 20% down and moved into their own home, Bill's first order of business was to build an antenna that would allow him to speak to anyone on the globe. Sandra would quell rumors in the neighborhood that Bill was actually some sort of operative for Germans or worse, the Ruskies, but secretly enjoyed the gossip. It was certainly more interesting than what he was actually doing, as far as she was concerned.

Over time, they did as married couples do and had four children, two boys and two girls. The boys were, of course, licensed hams as soon as they were old enough and pretended to share their dad's passion. The girls played violin and piano and later would get heavy into the gunge music scene from neighboring Seattle. They loved their dad for his endless selection of flannel shirts. He didn't like their music but did help them set up a small, semi-legal broadcast of the angsty songs. Both boys ended up in the Navy and both girls ended up in broadcast radio and Bill couldn't be prouder.

"Hey, Tina Fey! You're done! But next time, you get that flush. Your van is not self-cleaning oven, yeah?" I laugh and assure the man I will do just that.

***

DJ's hands are cautiously at ten and two and he checks each mirror twice. I'm proud of how seriously he's taking safe driving. I remember when I met his dad and he was a new driver and he was the same way, checking every little thing twice. He looks so much like his father.

"Oh, look! Pancake House! Do you want to stop and grab a bite?" It was his favorite when he was young. We've completed his appointment at the doctor's and are headed back to the high school.

"Mom, I have an algebra test. You said I would be back by 4th period." He is stone cold and serious. I guess I should be grateful he takes after his dad in that way too. I couldn't have cared less about school, especially math.

"Of course, sorry. I just…" I trail off. Something catches my eye. A woman and a younger man pass by on the sidewalk in front of the Pancake House. They catch my eye; they look as if they're heading to a pride parade. The woman, in both a rainbow striped cardigan and dress, has her arm around the shoulder of the man in jeans and a rainbow pride t-shirt. They both have brightly striped sunglasses on and matching red sneakers. They both look as if they're terribly upset, the boy visibly crying.

It's September, an absurd time to celebrate pride with this much enthusiasm. Why would they be dressed like this? Why are they so sad?

Her name is Isabelle and the young man is her son. She had him terribly young, 16-years-old. She named him River because she was too young to understand the complications of naming a child something unusual. When her son was almost a year old, his father came out. He was the same age, now 17, and had found himself. He was apologetic to Isabelle but had to live his true life. She wasn't all that surprised. They'd met when they were both in the school musical and he taught her how to do stage makeup.

River's dad, Gabriel, promised to still be a dad. His visits went from once a week to once a month as he got more involved in the 'scene' and started drinking heavily on a fake ID in the clubs. Isabelle internally knew eventually she would need to do this all on her own, so she asked her parents to fund her going to dental hygienist school. By the time she was 19, she had a good job and an apartment of her own and paid for her son's expensive pre-school without any help. She asked Gabriel to watch River so she could go out on her 20th birthday, but he was going to New York's famed Fire Island for the summer with his much older boyfriend.

Gabriel would oscillate between involved and absent over the years. He was the proudest papa at kindergarten graduation, receiving praise and adulation for playing piano at the event and staging pictures with a borrowed professional camera. It would take Isabelle nearly a year to get the actual photographs from Gabriel, which would be the next time the man would see his son.

When River was 10, Gabriel moved to Los Angeles with dreams of working as a choreographer. Isabelle was still happily working in Seattle, saving for a condo all her own. After being priced out for yet another barely big enough unit, she started looking in Eastern Washington. Her parents had retired in the touristy Leavenworth, and she always loved the area. Within a month she's secured a great job and modest home in Wenatchee, just 30 miles away from her parents. Gabriel tried to protest, but he'd already left the state altogether. They made plans for River to visit for two whole weeks when Gabriel had settled into a bigger place.

That never happened.

Gabriel came back to Seattle when River was 12. Isabelle learned about this on facebook. She arranged a weekend visit, Gabriel staying with her and River. She needed to see him, she'd been seeing a man for a year at this point and she wanted to introduce him to River, but it felt wrong to do so without at least a discussion with the boy's father. At first, Gabriel was frantic, feeling replaced but was reasonable, if not disappointed in his own actions toward the boy. Over the next year, Gabriel kept to a regular visitation schedule and became an important part of the boy's life. He stopped drinking and started working with an organization in Seattle that aided unhoused LGBTQ youth. He and his boyfriend had a great apartment on Pine St. and River stayed over every other weekend. Isabelle was thrilled they were developing a close relationship. Although her own relationship didn't work out, she enjoyed getting some time to herself and started looking into furthering her career into medical office management. She also started kick-boxing regularly and felt physically great.

Seemingly out of nowhere, Gabriel canceled his weekend with no real reason. It would be two months until Isabelle and River heard from him. He was back in New York; he and his boyfriend had a rough breakup and he was staying with friends. He was clearly drunk when he called.

He would drunkenly call every few months, promising a visit, apologizing for being absent. River grew angry and refused to talk to his father after a while. Isabelle was unsure what to do. Gabriel needed help. Months became years. The phone calls stopped and she would see pieces on social media, club photos and trips to the north shore. River started kick-boxing too and it proved an excellent way to work out his anger. And Isabelle grew close to the kick-boxing instructor and when you know, you know, and they had a small spring wedding. River gave his mom away and the now 15-year-old was thrilled for his mother's happiness and adored his step-father.

The three of them went on adventures to Costa Rica and Iceland. They tried to meet up with Gabriel in New York during a layover, but he flaked. Gabriel eventually grew comfortable with video-calling his son with some regularity. He was still drinking a lot and partying more, but had settled into a happy life in New York. The two made vague plans about River visiting that would never materialize. Gabriel became obsessed with River's graduation from high school the next year. He was absolutely certain he would come for the ceremony and take pictures.

Time marched on and one day Isabell received a call from a hospital in New York. Gabriel was sick, gravely sick and had listed her as his emergency contact. She asked the nurse if she and River should fly out, if they even had the time to do so. She implied it would be a matter of days, so Isabelle booked two spendy tickets and left within hours. River was stoically silent, unsure how to feel.

Gabriel was emaciated and covered in tubes and wires; his once bright eyes dulled with sickness. Pancreatitis, a near-certain death sentence for advanced HIV/AIDS. They had no idea he was sick. Perhaps he didn't know. He was heavily medicated for the pain, but would have moments of clarity between doses and used the time to frantically apologize to his son. The boy, showing his earned maturity, held his dad's hand and told him all was forgiven and shared good memories. It was heartbreaking to all who could witness, Isabelle having to leave the room to fall apart. Once, while River stepped out to use the bathroom, Isabelle asked Gabriel what he wished for his remains and services. Gabriel laughed and said he wanted the two of them to throw the tiniest pride parade and spread his ashes somewhere beautiful. He said he wanted her to play the music from Once Upon a Mattress, the musical where they had met.

Gabriel passed early the next morning. The last words he spoke were telling River that having a son was the best thing he'd done with his life.

The nurses carefully packaged Gabriel's belongings and handed them to Isabelle. She signed paperwork to have him cremated. The two used clues from Gabriel's belongings to figure out where he'd been living and found his roommates, breaking the sad news. They surrounded the two in love and hugs and showed the boy Gabriel's room - covered in pictures and mementos of his estranged son. They encouraged River to take whatever he wanted. Isabelle gave him privacy to explore while she made arrangements with the crematorium and airlines. She never asked what the boy took and they returned to their lives in Washington.

Isabelle had purchased the brightest, gayest clothes she could find for the pair and picked a gorgeous autumn morning to have their private memorial. They spread Gabriel at their favorite river bank and got pancakes after.

"Mom?" DJ sighs. "Mom, we're here. I have to go now." He's impatient. I wipe a tear from my eye and tell him to have a good day.

***

I chastise myself for allowing my stupid day dreaming to distract me while DJ was driving. I don't even remember arriving at the high school. What if he'd caused an accident? I check my to-do list and I have an hour to kill before my personal appointment with the lady doctor. It's time for my annual pap and titty check. What fun.

Spontaneously, I decide to kill that time over at my husband's clinic. It's across the street from the hospital and maybe if I bring food to him, he'll have a few minutes to enjoy it with me. I swing through the Wendy's drive thru and get two salads and two diet cokes. Something nags at me as I enter, he doesn't seem to like surprises. Marcy greets me at the front desk with a curious smile. I show her the bags of food and tell her I'm hoping to snag a 10-minute lunch with Danny. She looks over his schedule and makes a face. He's in back-to-back appointments until late afternoon. I shrug and assume this is what I get for thinking. I leave the salad with Marcy and think about asking her to ask him for a quick hug before I go, but can't stand the possibility of seeing her pitying face relaying that rejection.

***

I eat my Wendy's salad in my van in the parking lot. I park far away so no one can see my shame. I even ordered the grilled chicken instead of the vastly superior breaded and fried, hoping to please my husband. Look, Danny, I can eat healthy too. Look Danny, I am fun and spontaneous and maybe you should pay a little more attention to me.

I stop myself. That's not fair. Daniel is a wonderful husband. He's never been very showy or egregious with his affection, but he's so very tender and loving when we're alone. He's an amazing father to our sons. He's an excellent provider; we want for nothing in this world. He's got excellent hygiene. I hear women complain about that sometimes, their husbands not smelling all that good - Daniel always smells as if he's freshly showered, even right after work.

I realize I'm being watched. There's a person in the manicured bushes surrounding the parking lot of the hospital. It breaks my heart; Wenatchee's homeless population seems to have doubled or tripled in the last few years. The man is filthy, in torn baggy clothes surrounded by several bags and a small cart. I can't believe I was so distracted by my thoughts I didn't see him at all. I pretend to look at my phone to break the awkward eye contact we have. I sneak a peek and he's looking away now. How does one get to this place? We have shelters. I know they're not the best but it's got to be better than hiding in bushes.

I'm sure that's just my privilege talking. I read a great article on the unhoused community in HuffPo, many are turned away from shelters due to mental illness, criminal history, or addiction. I bet that's it. He looks like a drinker. I know a drinker when I see one. My father is a red-nosed lush.

This man's name is Wally and he's either 57 or 58 years old. He heard his mother put his birth year at 1960 sometimes and 1961 others. She once told him it was so he could start kindergarten early but that didn't make any sense because he was the oldest in his class. Well, he was until he dropped out in eighth grade. Wally had a regular gig as a bar back, at first to pay back his mother's tab at the waterfront tavern and then they kept him on. He made enough to give his mom ten dollars a week and keep her off his ass about school. Wally hated school. Wally hated pretty much everything.

Except comics. His job allowed him to keep up with all the DC and Marvel comics he could ever want to buy. Sometimes, when he knew no one would see him, he drew his own comics. He developed a character that had the ability to manipulate matter itself. MatterMan could do basically anything: shape shift, turn dirt into gold, cure cancer, anything you can think to do. But, like all comic heroes, he had an Achilles heel - he was only powerful for short bursts and then without any power at all. He had a little warning; he could feel himself draining and he would have to find somewhere safe to hide while he recharged.

Wally never had the courage to show anyone his drawings or ideas. He'd only been told he was useless and stupid his whole life and he didn't want to give anyone more to hold against him.

After his mama died, he bounced from bar to bar, working a few weeks and then drinking away his whole paycheck. Somewhere near Tulsa he lost his identification and was afraid to renew it due to outstanding warrants - mostly drunk and disorderly charges. Wally wasn't sure if he was afraid of jail or the withdrawals he'd suffer in jail. That put an end to legitimate work; Wally stuck to labor jobs and panhandling.

Wally knew love once. Somewhere around St. Louis he'd picked up a traveling partner, a pretty lady who loved wine. Her name was Abigail and she had the prettiest eyes he'd ever seen. She was kind and simple and Wally loved her madly. They'd found a flop house to survive the brutal Missouri winter and the boss-man took a liking to Abigail. He'd make jokes about stealing her away, or killing Wally. They didn't feel like jokes. Abigail wanted to leave but Wally knew they'd never find anything this safe and warm for the two of them. Wally went to the boss and told him he'd step away if the bossman promised to keep Abigail in wine and never, ever hit her. He knew she'd be better off with him. He made love to her one last time and headed to Oregon for the weather and he'd heard rumors of free dental clinics.

Wally isn't exactly sure how he ended up in Wenatchee or how long he'll stay. The view is pretty and there's plenty of free meals at the many, many churches. Washington legalized weed and folks sure are generous with it. Wally doesn't really make plans; he likes to let fate decide.

Oh, fuck, my appointment.

***

"Hi, there," I started apologetically. "I'm Nancy Caulkins. I have a 2:00PM with Dr. Sheridan." I lean in and softly confess, "I'm a little late."

"Hi Nancy," The sweet-faced receptionist greets me. I don't think I've met this one yet. I wonder how long she's worked here. I've seen Dr. Sheridan for nearly 20 years and seen so many sweet-faced young girls in this seat. She hands me a clipboard and says the doctor will be right with me.

Chapter 3:

"So, what's new?" Dr. Sheridan is so casual about these things. She's opening my vaginal canal to swab my cervix and acting as if we're in line for the ATM. I'm never comfortable in the stirrups and I think she can tell.

"Nodda lotta." I match her informality. "Actually," I start but I don't know how to say I'll find the courage.

"Actually what?" She asks simply. "It's ok, Nan. You can ask me anything. Is it about discharge?"

"No." I'm suddenly able to speak and I feel my face go red. I take a deep breath. "Am I, perhaps, nearing, you know, the change?" I almost whisper the last part.

"Not even close." She doesn't hesitate. "Are you experiencing symptoms of menopause or perimenopause?"

"I'm not sure." I'm really not. My mother died at 36, when I was 16-years-old. My grandmother died young too. I have no close aunts or friends in that age group. I've never witnessed the change, only what I've read and seen in movies.

"Well, what makes you ask that?" She is finished and taps my knee, the universal invitation to sit back up. I sit but say nothing.

"Nan, I have been seeing you for nearly 20 years. I delivered your babies. Tell me what's going on."

I think over the two decades I have known Dr. Sheridan. All the different times I've wondered about her personal life. I've imagined her to be a lesbian in a relationship with a woman who has hundreds of plants and wears long cotton dresses. I've pegged her to be a secretive biker, spending weekends on her Harley in a vest covered in patches. I once fully believed she was an escapee of a fundamentalist cult. She's a tiny woman, barely over five feet and rail thin who always wears her hair in edgy, short haircuts. Other than her occupation for her entire adult life, I know next to nothing about the woman.

She's looking at me expectantly. I take a deep breath. "I guess maybe I should see my regular doctor. It's probably not a reproductive health issue."

"Nan, you can talk to me. What's up?"

"I daydream too much. I always have but lately it's much worse. I feel…" I'm unsure how I feel about it, honestly. I've always liked my vivid fantasies. "I feel like maybe it's holding me back a bit. I know it's not normal."

"Everyone daydreams, Nancy. You're normal. But if you feel like you're having sudden focus issues, that can be age related or a sign of something else. Let's set up appointments with your primary care and a psychiatrist."

Great, she thinks I'm crazy. I shouldn't have said anything. "No, no. I'm sure it's nothing to worry about. I'm fine really."

"Nancy, there's no shame in getting checked out. This is likely nothing, but it doesn't hurt anything to run some tests and see, ok?" She's already writing something down. Great, this is on my permanent record.

***

Last couple items on my to-do list: I need thread to sew DJ's patches on his Boy Scout's uniform and I need to hit the bank. I'm 3 or 4 patches behind, I ran out of the specific tan color needed. I love the fabric store; I love wandering the aisles of interesting patterns and sumptuous textures. JoAnne's is back on the east side of town but the only other option in town is one: also on the east side and two: the place that I dare not shop as I believe in reproductive rights.

As I pulled out of JoAnne's Fabrics, I noticed a man walking: very tall, long beard, and an eye patch. This man was very recognizable. I pondered why he wore an eye patch for a few minutes as I drove to the bank. When I exited the bank, I saw the same man. I was curious how he'd gotten so far on foot, but shrugged it off. I never walk anywhere so how would I know how long it takes. I may have been in the bank longer than I thought, too. I crossed the intersection to Safeway, did some last-minute grocery shopping and saw the same man sipping a coffee at their Starbucks.

Immediately, my weirdo brain thinks he must be following me. I relax, it was just across the street, and it's not like there's many places to go in East Wenatchee. Then my brain goes into overdrive about this man's life and speculates how he's gotten to where he is today. He's older so his name is likely John, James, William, or Ronald. I decide James, like his father, but everyone called him by his middle name Edward, or Eddie to those who call him friend.

Eddie was born in Colorado, to upper lower-class parents. The kind of people that vote republican because they believe in small government and think that's what it means. His parents genuinely loved their only son and his father rarely ever gave him the belt. His mother was an excellent cook and struggled to keep little Eddie in long enough pants, the boy was ever-growing. He joined the Coast Guard at 18 because they didn't care about his grades and being land-locked his whole life, he was desperate to experience the ocean. He loved the Coast

Guard life and became a knowledgeable and needed sailor quickly. He'd always been good with his hands and they trained him in boat mechanics. As the cold didn't bother him, he was stationed in Alaska and perfectly happy with a nightlife of low-lit bars, hefty women, and over-priced blended grain whiskeys.

Eddie never really talks about the night he lost his eye. He let his family assume it had happened in the line of duty and never corrected them. To this day only four people know the whole truth: Eddie, a generous woman named Belinda, Belinda's husband, and the doctor who treated both men. The incident excluded him from service, so he joined up with a small but profitable commercial fishing vessel. He happily fished for the next 20 or so years until his arthritis sent him in search of a more tepid, forgiving climate.

Somewhere on his way to visit Colorado, he landed in Wenatchee for a night. He liked our mountains and our sun, the agreeable rent prices, and the cheerful, likable townsfolk. He's semi-retired here, living off savings and a part-time gig with the local boat store. East Wenatchee PD popped him for DUI seven years ago and he decided to give up driving altogether, walking keeps him fit. He's as happy as he can be here without his life-long love: the ocean.

"Ma'am? Are you okay?" Oh damn. It's the same kid as last time I did this. The same under-paid courtesy clerk, sent to check on the catatonic middle-aged mom, frozen on the baking aisle.

"I hope so, kid. Thanks."

***

Back home, I throw some salmon under the broiler while I toss a salad. Look at me, the picture of health: two salads in one day. I text Daniel, asking when he thinks he may be home. DJ has Scouts tonight and I've already sewn his patches and pressed his uniform. He's set a goal to make Eagle like his father and is very close. DJ pops his head in the kitchen and makes a face.

"Gross! I hate fish." He laments.

"That's weird, you like fish sticks." I chuckle. I mouth along as he claims, "That's different."

"I'll throw some chicken nuggets in for you." I assure him as I reach into the freezer. At that moment my phone rings. I smile, thinking maybe it's Danny on his way home - unable to text. Unfortunately, it's my sister. She only calls when she needs money or a baby-sitter. Usually both.

"Hey Candace." I answer. I'm careful with my tone. She's my baby sister, only five when our mom died. I was basically her only parent as our dad completely checked out after he lost his wife. I love her, but she can be draining. I hear crying in the background. She has two girls, ages three and four, both are a handful.

"Hi Nan. I wouldn't ask but I have a shift at the bar tonight and no sitter. Their dad bailed again. Can you watch them?"

I roll my eyes. Her ex-boyfriend is such a piece of shit. I don't know why she ever thinks she can count on him. "We have Scouts tonight; Deej is presenting his Eagle project. I don't want to miss it."

"You can take the girls with you! They would love that." She's grasping at straws. She knows her terrorist toddlers would spend the whole time whining and crying.

"What about the neighbor?" Candy has an older neighbor lady that actually likes the girls. She's a retired teacher and the go-to sitter in their apartment building.

"I feel bad, I owe her money from last time." Candace confesses.

"How much? I can drop off some cash; I went to the bank today." I really don't want to deal with my nieces tonight.

"Forty. Well, actually, I owe her for the last two times so $80." A screaming deal as far as I'm concerned. "I can pay you back." She and I both know she won't. I agree and tell her I will drop it off as soon as I can.

"Hey, if you have it," She continues, "Can you throw in an extra ten for smokes?"

***

The 20 minutes before bed is my favorite time on earth. Daniel and I take turns at the sink, brushing our teeth. I take care of my face and then we help each other apply lotion to our backs. We both suffer dry skin and the routine, born out of necessity, thrills me every time. I love running my hands down his body and I get goosebumps from feeling his. We usually chat a little about our day and decompress.

While he expertly runs his hands down my back, I gaze at him in the mirror. He's so handsome. I capture his hands and wrap them around my front. I lean into his chest.

"Babe, do you ever daydream?" I ask him.

He laughs. "We both know you do. A lot."

"Yeah, but do you?"

"Sometimes." He kisses the side of my face and meets my gaze in the mirror. "I fantasize about you in that little black thing I got you for our anniversary." He raises his eyebrows. I grin and turn around to kiss him passionately.

I don't know why I get so in my head about my marriage, I think to myself as he leads me to our bed. We're just fine.

***

Today, I'd planned on cleaning out my van and organizing the garage a little. I asked for helper volunteers and wouldn't you know my sons and my husband have plans. Shocking, I know. I'm in yoga pants and Danny's tattered university sweatshirt and despite looking like fresh garbage, I feel amazing. Glowing from last night, I tackle my tasks with enthusiasm and 90's R&B.

I pull a box off the storage shelf to sort. It's unlabeled and dusty, probably sitting here - untouched - for the decade we've lived here. I unfold the top and see my high school yearbook. Ambitions for productivity are immediately cast aside and I sit on the garage floor with the tome.

I find myself first, remembering the awful bangs I thought would somehow work with my curly hair. I grin when I find Danny. This is our senior year and we're dating at this point. My friend Shari Koonz really wanted to go on a date with Daniel's friend Jake and had suggested we double. She was Mormon and not allowed to go out with Jake alone. Shari and Jake never saw each other again but Daniel and I got along well and he asked me out again. And again, and again.

I haven't talked to Shari in years. She's in Arizona and I see on facebook she manages a clothing shop. She seems happy. Jake and Daniel still meet for basketball or the occasional Seahawks game.

Next to Shari's picture I see Kacey Kraft. I didn't know her but I loved her name. Alliteration is great. I used to say her name silently when I saw her in the halls. I secretly envied Kacey Kraft. She was everything I wished I could be. She had piercings and brightly colored hair and wore spiked collars and giant boots. I heard a rumor that she was a lesbian but I also heard a rumor that she was dating a drummer that had already graduated. When she wasn't at school anymore, I heard she had dropped out, that she had run away, and that she was in juvie.

I bet she did run away. She left on tour with her drummer boyfriend, Keefer. With nothing in their pockets, the band had a van and a dream and exactly one groupie/merch girl. They hit Portland first where they had a couple guaranteed gigs. Over the next year Kacey lived on vodka and cigarettes. She got dangerously skinny but also learned how to play the drums almost as well as her teacher. One night, Keefer was too drunk to go on and the band let Kacey play instead. After this happened a dozen or so times, they left Keefer in some random town in Mississippi and continued to tour with Kacey.

She would go on to band hop a bit before conceptualizing her own band. Death Rays to Cuba was an all-girl ska-punk band that reached relative success in the New England underground punk scene. At the height of her career, the band opened for Pennywise and once played at a Tony Hawk video game launch party.

Tired of the road, Kacey and her bassist opened a small music shop in Connecticut, placating Ivy League kids who want to feel edgy. Kacey will never marry but has a boyfriend named Zero and a girlfriend named Jenna. Some nights she'll hit an open mic and perform twee covers of punk songs on her ukulele, some nights she goes to the punk-show and punches a guy in the throat for no real reason. She's the happiest and healthiest she's ever known.

Kacey Kraft. Man, I would love to know her.

Shit. My legs are asleep. How long have I been sitting here? I look at my phone. I've missed three calls from my dad. I sigh deeply. Oh, it's going to be one of those days. Must be the fifth of the month.

***

"Oh, Nanny, down from the heights, gracing her old father with a visit." My father sneers. "Aren't you afraid to park your car in this neighborhood?" It's the house I grew up in, a modest ranch-style in a working class but completely safe part of town.

"You said you needed help." I'm not taking his bait today. "If you're going to be a dick, I can leave. Maybe Candy can help you."

"The whore? She can't count." Again, I don't take the bait. He wants me to argue, to put up a fight. And then if I get mad, he wins. I learned this ages ago. He's called my sister the whore since she had her first daughter without being married. I wonder what he calls me when I'm not around.

I wait. He finally hands me a stack of mail. Alcoholism has destroyed my father on many levels. I'm not sure if it's the reason behind his poor vision or if that's standard old man problems. He can't see his bills to pay them. His pension and social security both come on the fifth of the month and he's eager to pay his bills to know how much he has left to drink. He'll have plenty, he always does. His pension from driving city buses for 45 years is generous and he's paid off the house. I walk over to the small console table by his easy chair for his check book and registry. We've been in this habit for years: me coming over once a month to pay his bills and balance his checkbook. Sometimes I clean a little, but the old man keeps care of himself and the house just fine.

"Your grandson's Eagle Scout project was approved. He's going to build a new swing set for the park by the river." I idly catch him up on the boys' accomplishments and growth. Daniel made a rule ages ago that my father wasn't allowed around my sons when he was drinking so they hadn't seen their grandfather but once or twice in the last few years. He listens half-heartedly while watching some talk show.

I focus on television as well. It's the one show where four women meet daily and film their opinions on current events and interview pop stars. The cast has changed and I only recognize two of them. I hardly ever watch any TV. Or really watch movies. I'm so busy with the kids and can never seem to focus on anything longer than a few minutes. I try to listen to audiobooks when I can. They're interviewing an actress and

I think I do recognize her. A brash blond with a loud laugh who starred in those movies about kids having to battle to the death. DJ enjoyed those films, insisting he catch them in the theatre.

An hour later, my father's finances are squared away and I'm desperate to leave. I hate this house now. Dad hasn't so much as moved a piece of furniture since mom died and what once felt like a touching memorial now feels like a tomb in the making.

***

When I return home, there's a man sitting on the flower bed bricks in my front yard. I debate on if I should go ask him if he wants something and see he's got a guitar in his hands. I open my kitchen window and soft music floods in. He's an older Latino man, in simple but clean work clothes. Deciding he's harmless, I just stand there and enjoy my private troubadour.

I name him Francisco and speculate how he came to be in this moment my personal concerto. He's a petite man, likely from Central Mexico. His family comes up every year for Wenatchee's bustling harvest season. He's happy to pick our fruit, earn some cash, and go home to play guitar in small venues and parties. Francisco likes a simple life, never seeking anything extravagant. As long as he's got something to make music with and food in his belly - he's a happy man.

He was the second youngest of five kids. His mother is an incredible cook and still wipes his face like he's a child. His oldest brothers are in transportation and urged him to drive the big trucks as well, but driving always made Francisco nervous. To this day, with 55 years of life lived, he's never actually driven any vehicle. He has a wife and two now grown kids and they can drive him anywhere that's too far to walk.

His love of walking is how he ended up in front of my house today. The agricultural housing is about three miles away, but he saw a crow fly this way and he wanted to see where he was heading. He's got the day off; the crew is waiting for more boxes. He followed the crow for a while but lost him somewhere on 5th St. Then he heard rhythmic pounding of the men working on Western and wanted to see what they were up to. The beat put a song in his heart and he walked until he saw somewhere quiet to sit and now he's composing a musical love letter to this moment. To him, everything, every atom of every particle we can see, feel, hear, or taste, is sheet music to the score of life.

Francisco has always lived this way, letting the universe decide which direction to head, hearing her song and translating it the best he can.

I'm awed by the philosophy of this man. I wish I could see the world the way he does.

I don't have time for that. I quietly close the window and return to decluttering the garage.

***

Why are all waiting areas burgundy and hunter green? At some point was there a study that said these two colors are the best choices for people to wait to see their doctor? I shift my legs on the mildly uncomfortable vinyl seat and look over to the oak end table to see what magazines they have to offer. There's Golf Digest or Highlights - no thanks. I check my phone instead. I'm halfway into a BuzzFeed quiz on what my breakfast order says about my personality when my name is called. I'm seeing my primary care physician for the first time in years. I'm healthy; I've been fortunate enough to not have a reason to come in.

My doctor is, well, uninteresting. He's a generic, middle-aged, white man in a lab coat. He looks exactly like what would come up if you googled 'doctor'. He looks at my chart on a laptop atop a rolling cart and asks why I'm in today. I'd follow through with my ObGyn's advice to make sure I don't have a brain tumor or some sort of day-dreaming psychosis.

"I'm not sure. I seem to be having trouble with focus." I inform him.

"Okay. That's not uncommon. Especially with women your age." He looks at the screen again. "I see you were medicated for postpartum depression after your second son was born." I take a deep breath at the memory. That was an incredibly difficult time for me. I couldn't stop crying, couldn't sleep. I had no idea what was wrong with me. I loved little baby Patrick, but I was miserable. Fortunately, Dr. Sheridan saw the symptoms and put me on a mild dose of Celexia and I felt better in a few weeks. I stayed on it, precautionarily, for a year and eased off.

"Yes," I try not to sound defensive. "It's common and temporary. I'm not depressed now."

"Depression is also common in women your age and can present in unexpected ways - such as inability to focus or 'brain fog' as they call it. I would like to refer you to a psychiatrist."

"I came in to make sure I don't have a brain tumor. I'm not depressed." I am definitely defensive now.

"Nancy, can I call you Nancy?" He continues without waiting for a response, "You don't have any other symptoms consistent with a brain tumor or any other brain traumas. Are you hallucinating?" Again, he doesn't wait for a response. "Are you blacking out for chunks of time? No. It's probably mild depression. Most adults have it. You'll see Dr. Harris; she'll get you on Prozac or Lexapro and you'll feel better and experience less dysfunction in your day-to-day life." He's already completing the referrals on his screen and signing off on the appointment before I can have a chance to even think of what to say.

***

I dislike the look of cargo shorts. I see a man wearing them on the sidewalk. He was of medium height, a bit stout/hearty, with a neatly trimmed VanDyke and a belt clip for his enormous cell phone. How and why had man come to be on South Chelan Ave. in Wenatchee, WA, on this specific Tuesday afternoon?

He looked to be no older than 30; I'd say he was 28 - he had the stride of a man who's never pulled a gray out of his pubes but has bitched about income taxes. That means he's an Andrew or Tyler or, no, he's a Nicholas. But only his mother and big sisters call him that - to everyone else he's just Nick. He's the guy you call when you need to borrow his truck or want company for a domestic beer. Salt of Earth Nick, always jovial and a bit loud and rowdy but rarely, if ever, unkind.

Nicholas David Granier was born to Ellen and Floyd Granier in the early 90s. He was child number three of four, and the only boy. Floyd wasn't a jerk about his house of mostly girls, though, he was a tech guy in the Seattle dot.com boom and working like a pack mule, too busy or tired for his family most of the time. Nicolas learned early the only attention he'd be guaranteed from Dad was when he caused trouble, so he was in the principal's office often. Nick was a sweet young man, but he fell in with the 'troubled' boys early and, well, being bad can be oh, so fun.

He had a huge crush on Amanda Lynn, a sandy blonde with a spiral perm and a baby blue retainer. He had just worked up the courage to ask her to go to the mall when she wasn't at school that day. Amanda's bestie told Nick she'd moved to the east side of the mountains with her family. He was crushed and a little quieter in class from then on.

Few people know the day their lives find purpose and direction. Nick is one of the few. He was in 11th grade, 17, and his metal shop teacher called him over and said the large equipment dealer was looking for a yard boy and the teacher had recommended Nick. Nick was to report to the dealership after school the next day in heavy boots and a can-do attitude. The yard was filled with steel beasts, earth movers and sky-lifts. Machinery that makes men Gods, with a little diesel and a basic understanding of physics. Nick was wowed. He was all the more impressed by the head salesman's brand new, candy apple red F250 custom extended cab. Nick found a mentor. Nick had a dream.

Years later, he saw on facebook that Amanda Lynn had moved to Wenatchee and her relationship status was single. Before he took his lunch break, he'd two interviews lined up in the Valley. He wasted no time and asked Amanda Lynn out while he was in town. A beer at Joe's would lead to four years of wedded bliss, a well-behaved black lab, and talk of children. She teases his shorts today as she had in 7th grade and they couldn't be happier.

The loud blare of honking rouses me from the immortal love story of Nick and Amanda-Lynn, the light has changed and the driver behind me furiously hitting his horn and flipping me off.

Chapter 4:

"Overall, you're good at what you do. I mean, it's not all that hard: answer the phone and file the reports, a monkey can do it. And you do fine." Frankie Jr. just compared me to a goddamn monkey in a performance review. The audacity of this man. "You are a little...I don't know how to say this, especially lately, you're flakey. People have to call your name a couple times before you answer. You stare off into the window like a house cat or something. It's weird. We need you to pay attention."

He pauses. He's looking for me to apologize, to promise to do better.

"I'm, um, actually being seen for that." I start. I do not want to tell this man my personal business. "My hearing." I lied. "I'm seeing a doctor about my hearing problems. That's why I don't always answer right away." I didn't know I could lie this well, on the spot. This is the perfect excuse, less embarrassing than 'Oh, I constantly daydream about strangers and make up wildly detailed backstories for them for no reason at all because I'm a fucking weirdo'.

"Oh." His tone changes. "Oh. Ok. Do you need a special phone or something?"

***

Returning to my desk, I am counting my breaths in and out. Inhale for four, hold for four, exhale for eight. Repeat. Some boujie shit I picked up in a yoga class or on Oprah or something, but it works. I will not cry at work. I cannot cry at work. I left the performance review informed that I did not meet the criteria for my annual raise. It's not about the money. Sometimes, I feel worthless.

I check the clock. Two hours and then I can leave. I can survive two hours. One hundred and twenty minutes. I check my email and then glance out the window. How many times has this window gotten me in trouble at work? I've always felt warmly about my daydreaming habit. I've liked trying to figure out the mysteries that lie beneath. But I can't help but think this may actually be a serious problem.

I bet she never daydreams. I see a woman, my age, in a smart blazer and skirt. It's eye-catching, a professional dark plum or eggplant. Aubrogene if you're clever. She looks so put-together. She's walking at a fast clip, obviously in a hurry to wherever she's headed. From the tailored professional clothes and her dark blond hair tied in a sensible French twist, I would say she's a divorce attorney headed to court.

She fights tirelessly for her clients. She's in a hurry now because she was just next door getting the information and informal testimony of the kid at the ice cream shop that witnessed her client's soon to be ex-husband slap her across the face. That will be exactly what her client needs to win custody of her kids. Alexa mostly deals in these sorts of messy, ugly divorces that would make most people run. She lives for it.

Alexa Dawn Adams didn't set out to be Wenatchee's top divorce lawyer. She didn't have much ambition at all, other than to get out of Miles City, Montana and away from her abusive step-father. She watched her mother, Joanna, go from a bright and funny mom to a withdrawn and lost widow to an abused, vacant wife in the span of three years. She tried often and energetically to encourage her mother to see how bad it was and leave. But the mother she so adored, the mother who constantly baked and fostered orphaned baby kittens and sang loudly and off key in the car - her mommy - was gone. When she graduated Miles City High School, she left the shell of Joanna Adams behind.

Alexa went to WSU in Pullman and was undeclared for the first year. She was thinking about communications or maybe business. She just wanted a career in anything where she could support herself and never, ever have to rely on a man. At the end of her freshman year, she read a story in the local paper about a man that killed his wife, their three children, and then himself after the wife tried to leave him and Alexa had a plan. She would help people leave abusive relationships and the best way to do that is legally. She declared pre-law and worked tirelessly hard to graduate at the top of her class. She was hired at Spokane's most prestigious law firm and earned a reputation for being a ruthless and effective advocate for her clients. She also adopted a tiny French Bulldog with a cleft lip named Roscoe and started working on healing the traumas from her past.

One day a woman timidly entered her office and explained that she needed to leave her husband but couldn't find a lawyer in her own town to represent her. The woman explained that her husband, when he wasn't beating her or cheating on her, was a county commissioner in Wenatchee and no local lawyer would come within 10 feet of her. Alexa not only represented that woman but also decided to move to Valley to open her own practice and break up the good ol' boys club that was Wenatchee's legal community.

Alexa walks past me with an ease and confidence I couldn't even imagine. I turn to grab today's comprehensive report from the printer and Frankie Jr and two other agents are watching me. Alexa wouldn't put up with this. Alexa would assertively ask them if they needed something and make them look away first. I'm no Alexa, sadly. I lower my head and try to focus on the report.

***

"Babe, have you seen my blue gym shorts?" Daniel is the mostly a perfect husband, but I swear sometimes he does treat me like his mother.

"Are they in your drawer?" I ask without looking or getting up. I'm trying to generate a meal plan and shopping list, looking at our family calendar. Much like most families, it's a constant battle to make all the pieces fit. "If they're not in your drawer, they're still in the dryer." He heads toward the laundry room. I notice that the boys have an overnight event this Friday. When Danny returns, I mention that we're completely free for a date night.

"That sounds good." He says. "Do you want to go to that Italian place or maybe sushi?"

I consider the options. I love both. However, something nags at me.

We're boring. I'm boring. He's boring. We always go to the same places; we don't try anything new.

"What about live music?" I offer. "I saw a flyer downtown for some band playing at The Bar." I wasn't being vague; Wenatchee has a popular bar downtown cleverly called The Bar.

"A bar?" He asks incredulously. "You want us to go to a bar?" I know why he's so confused. One of the reasons Danny and I chose each other was while all our friends experimented with drinking and bars, we'd made a decision to live completely sober lives early on. Daniel was raised in a Mormon family, and while he doesn't practice - he doesn't poison his body with drugs or alcohol. I attended a support group for children of alcoholics when I was younger and learned that my best chance of a healthy life was to never start drinking. Neither of us have ever had a drink in our lives.

"We can drink soda or water at a bar." We'd been to lounge-style restaurants and sports bars before. It's fairly easy to opt not to drink.

"Do you really like this band's music or something?" He's still confused.

"No, I don't even know what kind of music it is. I just…" I trail off, I don't want to offend him or hint to him that I'm possibly depressed or likely a mental-case and carefully continue, "I want to try something new."

"Go see a band." His lips are pursed in thought. "In a bar. Eh, why not? Happy wife, happy life." He kisses my cheek and checks his phone. "Gotta go babe. I'll be home about 6:30. Love you." He's almost to the door when he doubles back to grab his beloved blue gym shorts. He laughs again. "We're going to see a band at a bar! Crazy!" He kisses me again and heads out.

***

On my way to work, I make sure I park by where I'd seen the flyer for the band. It's a terrible design, barely legible. I take a picture of the sign and text it to Danny so he knows the info too. He sends me back three exclamation points. A man approaches and tacks a piece of paper to the other side quickly and moves on to the next post. I wait a moment and then check out what he's posting. It's a brochure for goat head awareness. They're common here, vile little things. They've ruined countless bike tires and get stuck to your shoes. I read this man has started a group to educate the public on them and a free service to remove them from your property. How on earth would anyone get this passionate over a weed?

Little Jimmy Delaney loved two things: his mother and rolling down the big hill behind his house. Oh, sure, in the winter he'd settle for sledding down it, but every single day Jimmy would climb the hill, lay on his side and let physics carry him back down. He loved how dizzy and light headed he would be at the end. He'd center himself and truck back on up. He would do tirelessly until his mother would call him in for lunch. After lunch, he'd take a bath and a nap and then it was time for dinner. The two would watch TV until Jimmy felt tired and she'd tuck him into his bed with dinosaur sheets and a Captain America comforter. Some days she'd sit in her lounge chair and cheer his rolling, some days she'd putter around in her flower bed and garden. The first time he ever heard her curse was at a patch of goat heads violating her goldenrod mums. It was a simple life, but they were happy.

Jimmy got older and rolling went from daily to once in a while to hardly ever. He still loved his mother, of course, but he made friends to ride bikes with and had homework, so he spent less and less time with her. She would still tuck him in every night, under the protection of Captain America. One night he told her he was too old to be tucked in and sent her away. He felt badly, but he was now 12 and it was time for her to see how grown he was.

The next morning a sheriff came into his classroom and called his name. His classmates woo'd and ooo'd as he gulped in fear. He was certain he'd been found out for the nudie mag he'd hidden by the beaver dam in the creek by his house. He didn't steal, he'd just found it and looked at it. He didn't mean any harm. A loud noise started in his ears as the sheriff said, "I'm sorry son; your mama was in a bad car accident. You need to come with me."

The noise continued at the hospital as a local preacher put his arm around his shoulders and told him to pray and stayed as the social worker called his Aunt and Uncle in Idaho. He still heard it as Little Jimmy watched men shovel dirt over his mother's simple, white casket. He tossed in some flowers from her garden and quietly sobbed, snot and tears meeting at his lip.

His Uncle brought him back home to pack up his room. He couldn't focus. He didn't want to be in this house without her. He just wanted the noise to stop. He ran to the side of the house and got on his bike and started riding as fast as he could, hoping to outrun the noise. His eyes blurred, he didn't see the patch of gravel at the turn and he spun out into a giant patch of goat heads. A part of him was convinced it was his mother punishing him for not wearing a helmet or leaving without telling Uncle Joe. He limped home, thorns stuck deeply into his knee.

Jimmy would finish school in Coeur D'Alene and wash out at basic training for the Army. He wandered directionless for a few years when his uncle told him he was old enough to inherit his mother's small estate. Uncle Joe was pretty smart with money and had invested proceeds from the sale of his sister's home and car. Jimmy had money to put a down payment on a house or go to school - enough to get a head start on life. He moved back to Wenatchee and took a job at a local nursery and greenhouse and purchased a tiny home with a large garden. When he hit 40 and the midlife existential crisis hit, he decided to start the Greater Wenatchee Anti-Goat Head Collision and man an army to exterminate the verdant menace in his mother's honor.

I smile at the brochure and turn to go to work.

Something literally stops me. My leg suddenly feels like it weighs a thousand pounds. I cannot lift it. The heaviness passes into my other leg. I am now a statue. My arms also feel weighted and my lungs start to feel compressed. A terrifying panic sweeps my whole body and I focus all my energy into staying on my feet. I take a deep breath and assess: this isn't an allergic reaction - nothing is hot or swollen; this isn't a heart attack - that starts in the arm or back. This has to be mental. I have friends with anxiety disorders, this sounds like what they experience. What could I be anxious about?

A couple more deep breaths and I manage to get myself to the brick wall of the coffeeshop. I lean against it, and take my phone out. I call Danny but it goes to voicemail. I don't have many other options but I don't know what to do. Or even how someone else could help me.

I do know I absolutely cannot go to work today. The thought of it makes my throat tense and feel strangled. I see a table and chair to my left, outdoor seating for the coffeeshop. I'm only a half a block from work but might as well be in another continent - the thought of walking there, of picking up my feet to go would be as preposterous as getting to Europe. A server comes out to take my order. I rarely drink coffee but something hot to drink would be nice right now. I order a cafe mocha and thank her. It was the perfect distraction.

I get my phone out again and dial Frankie's direct line. Calling the office line would be fruitless, I'm not there to answer. I get his voicemail and tell him I'm unable to come in today. That's the truth. I realize I probably should give a reason so I half-whisper 'female troubles' and know he won't question a thing. The same excuse I would use to get out of math class sometimes. I'm actually acting like a teenager, skipping class and lying. Might as well smoke a cigarette and go to the record store too.

The server returns. I see the outline of a Bic lighter in her pocket and ask her if I can buy a smoke.

***

I never told Danny I smoked in high school. Not a lot, a cigarette here or there. I stopped when I found out I was pregnant and craved them every now and then, but never acted on it. Today, I am a teenager. Today I don't care about lung cancer or Danny's opinion or if I get fired. My boss could literally walk out the office door and see me here, not sick, smoking and drinking a coffee. How would my son say it: IDGAF.

I pick up my coffee and notice my arm no longer feels heavy. In fact, my whole body feels light as a feather. I finish my coffee and grin at all that is possible. I am unburdened today. I cannot remember the last time I had this kind of freedom. I've got nothing on my schedule until making dinner and picking up the boys from soccer practice and mathletes. I count on my fingers; I have nine whole hours to do whatever I want.

But first I need to move my van from this block. I'm being capricious, not stupid.

***

I hum to myself as I make dinner. I'm still giddy from an incredible day. I'm making Danny's favorite: funeral potatoes and fried pork chops. I rarely make them together, they're so unhealthy, but today is a day for indulgences. Like the pack of cigarettes I purchased. I only smoked four and threw the rest away. Honestly, the last one made me feel sick and I got a little paranoid that someone may see me. Also, I treated myself to a new pair of jeans, super tight and ripped all over. I'm way too old for them, probably, but I always wanted to wear something like that. I also got a blouse to wear with them, cropped and fishnet underneath and metal chains closing the neck line. I had told the salesgirl at the shop in the mall I was going to a rock show and did she ever know exactly what I needed. I contemplated some thick-soled combat boots to complete the look, but I want to try something new, not scare my husband. My black high heels will be sexy and edgy.

Aside from the shopping and surreptitious smoking, it was just a great day. I got another cafe mocha and took it to the park to watch people, my favorite activity. I went to the local music shop and found a couple CDs of the band we're seeing Friday.

I loved looking at the instruments, the sleek, shiny guitars in every hue, the glossy brass horns. I felt as if I were in a gallery seeing fine art.

Of course, the day wasn't without hiccups. I actually was not as free and unscheduled as I had thought. My appointment with the physiatrist was this afternoon. I totally spaced until they called me. I rescheduled for an opening they have on Thursday morning and I'm excited to have another reason to ditch out on work. The music swells to the swinging horns section and I turn it up. I've brought my old high school boombox into the kitchen as I didn't have any other way to play a CD. This band, Exploiting Spinoza, is 3rd wave ska, according to the kid at the music shop. He also said they were 'dope' and he was jealous I was old enough to catch their show. I dance to the music in my socks in the kitchen and notice Patrick staring at me like I'd grown a second head. I wave for him to dance with me and he hesitates momentarily, however the infectious blare of the ska trumpet is irresistible.

***

"You seem different." Danny observes while I happily smooth our nightly lotion on his back.

"Yeah." I agree. "Just a really good day." I'm afraid to tell him more. I'm not sure if he'd understand why I did what I did today, especially the cigarettes. I realize in that moment; just how much I keep from my husband. I don't think I've ever told him how much I dislike my job. I don't think I've ever been honest with myself about it.

"I'm glad to hear it." He remarks on my good day. He turns to switch places with me. "You deserve good days, babe." He kisses my neck and I grin. A good day will now be a great night.

***

After we make love, I lay in our bed completely content. Danny breathes deeply beside me, either asleep or nearing it. I'm wide awake, thinking about the waitress at the coffee shop. She reminds me of my sister, a pretty, young girl who trusted the wrong man and now has to work twice as hard to earn a living.

I can't remember what her name tag said. Callie? No, it was more original than that - Calla. Her mother's favorite flower was the Calla Lily and she was inspired to name her baby girl after them. Calla was raised by a real, bona-fide hippie, spending the first decade of her life in a converted school bus, traveling from one barter fair to another. Her mother, Jipsea, sold tinctures and essential oils and little bags of 'herbs' to people she trusted. In the winter, they had some land near

Canada where her mother grew the 'herbs' and actual herbs and cooked up her potions for the season.

The two built a homestead when Calla was 10-years-old, as her mother worried for the girl coming to age without proper plumbing. No one should have to learn how to execute a tampon in a port-a-potty. Calla's mother's permissive parenting led to Calla moving out at fifteen with her boyfriend. Jipsea never liked the angry, young man, and Calla was headstrong and in love. Jipsea signed the papers for the two to marry the next year, trusting her daughter to make her own mistakes. She'd taught her beautiful, thoughtful daughter she had autonomy over her body and her fate, always.

Two years of less-than-blissful marriage later, Calla was done. She called the cops one night after he hit her and broke the mirror in the bathroom. While he was in jail, she moved all her stuff out and into her friend's apartment. She got a restraining order and will file for divorce soon. She works at the coffeeshop most days and is a catering waitress on the weekends. She illegally grooms dogs on the side and hopes to get certified someday. She is going to purchase a van and have a mobile dog grooming service called Groomer Has It and move back to her mother's homestead. Calla will set up her own yurt and grow her own gardens and live as her mother always has: happily without men.

I think about the man I saw at the park, walking twin King Charles Cavaliers with and wearing a sport coat, slacks, and a sweater vest. Wenatchee isn't stuffy or formal. It's uncommon to see a man that well-dressed on a random weekday in Riverfront Park. He was older, excellent posture but a bit of a limp or cadence interruption that happens with age and hip problems.

I named him Gregory, never, ever Greg. Gregory Eugene Deaver. Gregory grew up in Union Gap, just outside Yakima, Washington, a sleepy rodeo town with a large native and Latino population. His father managed a large cattle ranch and expected much from his oldest son, who despised the smell and excursion of cattle farming. Gregory loved musicals. His mother shared her favorite movies with him when he was little: Meet Me in St. Louis and An American in Paris and Gregory lived for the flash and spectacle. He started singing and dancing everywhere he went until one day his father hit him upside the head and scolded him for being 'faggy' in the feed store.

Gregory didn't know exactly what the word meant, but knew he probably was and it probably was going to be a problem. He hid his secrets as well as he could for years, until at 16 when his father's foreman caught him making out with the stable boy, Jose. Gregory was told to pack his bags and his mother, crying, handed him two hundred dollars.

Gregory hitch-hiked to New York City to become a Broadway star. His voice was okay, nothing outstanding, but he could dance well and was tall and handsome. He earned chorus work, enough to afford a room in a shitty boarding house and to keep himself fed and clothed. He loved being a part of any production and made a great group of friends. He worked on Broadway until fewer and fewer auditions panned out and he realized he was too old to be a chorus boy and not talented enough to be a lead. He phoned home to see if his mother was still alive and she encouraged him to come back to the ranch. His father had passed and she could use some company.

Gregory spent the next decade dutifully at her side. He used dating apps to find temporary love as needed - Gregory wasn't interested in relationships. That is until he met Mark, who lived a couple hours north in Wenatchee. When his mother passed, he quickly sold the ranch and Gregory and Mark got a riverfront condo and matching dogs. They're both active in the local theatre and love their dogs as their children.

I thought about the salesgirl at the clothing shop in the mall. It wasn't a store I usually shop at, geared more toward teens and young adults like her. I bet her name was Bailey or Dani, something androgynous. Bailey was kind to the middle-aged lady bumbling around her salesfloor. She had long, enviable, dark hair with bright purple at the ends. I wonder if I could pull that off.

Bailey works at the mall part time and goes to the community college. She's in the radiology tech program and should graduate this spring. Most of her classmates are in the program to acquire a certification for a job that pays well without the time and hardship of a four-year degree. Not Bailey. Bailey's little sister was born with a painful degenerative spine disorder and she required near constant imaging. As long as Bailey could remember, the rad-techs were the nicest, prettiest, funniest girls in the hospital. While doctors and nurses and Bailey's mom were hyper-focused on her little sister, the rad-techs would go out of their way to make sure Bailey was entertained and comfortable too.

Bailey drives a vintage Beetle that breaks down every two weeks or so. She thinks it's sentient and waits for paydays.

My thoughts are interrupted by my alarm. Jeez. I don't think I slept at all. But I don't feel tired. I don't have to go to work today, I told Frankie I had back-to-back appointments all day for my hearing. The truth is I just have the make-up appointment with the psychiatrist and don't want to go to work after. I don't know if I ever want to go to work again.

Chapter 5:

I leave early for my appointment. I want to get a coffee and maybe sneak one more cigarette. I don't want this to be a habit, but they just feel so good.

I feel good. The giddiness from the day before lingers in my sleepless body. I'm considering making an appointment to get purple in the ends of my hair like Bailey, or maybe teal. I wonder if I can get in before Friday to complete my rock-n-roll look for Friday's show. I can't wait to see Daniel's reaction.

I'd never been to this part of the hospital before. It's on the same campus, but with a different entrance on the side street. Parking is easier and the aesthetic is different. The building is newer and made with sleek metals and dark woods. I found Dr. Harris's office with ease and check-in with her receptionist. They had said to come early for paperwork and they aren't lying, she hands me a loaded clipboard and I find a seat in the modern, sleek waiting area. Much nicer than my primary care, this looks like a hotel lobby.

I sign the release forms and consent and insurance things and am faced with a questionnaire.

How often do you have trouble wrapping up the final details of a project once the challenging parts have been done? I check 'sometimes' but realize it's likely more an 'often' or 'very often'. My garage is still a complete mess and I've had over a week. *How often do you have problems remembering appointments or obligations?* Well, I am here today because I completely forgot I had the last appointment so, yeah, 'often'.

This first one seems to be some sort of ADD/ADHD screening. That's interesting, I could see where that might be my problem.

I move to the next, clearly depression screening questions. I am careful with these, answering as honestly as possible. I move on to the last two, asking more generic questions about if I hear voices or see things that aren't there. Nothing really applies to 'daydreams so often I get in trouble at work and burn the garlic bread'. I return the paperwork and wait.

***

Dr. Harris is tiny, of Asian descent with gorgeous eyes and thick black hair. I am instantly charmed by her warm smile and calm, even voice. There's no couch, just two leather, side-armed chairs with a little table between. She gestures for me to sit in the one by the door. She gets right to business. "It says you're here because of excessive daydreaming and fantasies. Is that correct?" I nod. "Can you please tell me more about that?"

"I guess I just get really curious about people's backstories. Why they are who they are, where they are. So I see a person and try to figure it all out based on what I can see." I had never explained it so clearly to someone else before. I had mentally practiced that all morning.

"That doesn't seem dysfunctional, Nancy. I think a lot of people do that." She pauses. "Are these people you know or people you just see in public?"

"Mostly strangers. Or like, a neighbor I don't really know. My son Patrick's soccer coach. People like that." I guess it doesn't sound all that crazy when I think about it.

"Okay, thank you. Let's go over what your day-to-day life looks like. Would you call yourself a happy person? Do you ever get anxious or nervous over small things?"

"I am actually really happy." I smile. "I have a wonderful husband and two amazing sons." She checks the paperwork on her lap. "Daniel is my husband. My sons are DJ - Daniel Junior, but we call him DJ and Patrick. I work for an insurance company downtown, but consider myself a mom first. The boys are active in Scouts and soccer and school so I'm always busy and involved in all that."

"You sons..." She pauses and looks at another paper in my chart.

"Are you looking for the time I was medicated for postpartum depression? I had the baby blues, nothing abnormal." I get nervous, suddenly anxious. "I'm not depressed anymore. Really."

"Of course, Nancy. It's too early to diagnose anything. Tell me more about your relationship with your sons." She is still calm and even and looks up at me with a slight smile.

"Oh, I could brag for ages. DJ is so serious and driven. Honor roll student and about to start his Eagle Scout project. He's in advanced math and will be driving soon. Patrick, my little Patty-Cake is a soccer star and more fun and goofier. Just last night he danced in the kitchen with me to a new band I discovered." I laugh slightly. "They're such good boys."

"I see." She looks over her clock. "Nancy, you talking about your sons makes me realize I forgot to tell the school that my son has a dentist's appointment and I need to call them. I know this is terribly unprofessional, but would you mind?"

"Oh, please, do what you have to do!" I interrupt. "I totally understand." She gives me the 'one minute' gesture and goes toward her reception area. I look at the decorations on her wall. It's minimalist, just three wall hangings but lovely. A tree in the meadow in three parts, each a different season. I've seen these before and think they're clever. Dr. Harris returns and apologizes again. I remind her that it isn't a big deal.

"My forgetfulness is one of the reasons I am here." I chuckle.

"Tell me about the most recent daydream you've had. When was it and what inspired it?"

"I actually had a few last night and this morning. The last was about a girl who helped me pick out some clothes the day before. I was inspired, oh, I don't know, I liked her hair and she was very kind to me."

"What did you fantasize about her?"

"I don't think fantasize is the right word. That makes it feel lurid or gross." I am a little uneasy at the implication.

"What did you think about when you were thinking about her?"

Her eye contact remains steadfast.

"I was trying to think about what she's like, why she works there. Stuff like that." I have never had to explain this to another person. It's going to sound ridiculous.

"Nancy, I won't judge you. What did you think she was like?" She relaxes her posture a little and she waits for me to answer.

"I named her Bailey. She looked like a Bailey. She's going to school to be a radiology technician. She drives a bug and has a little sister." I could give more detail but I still feel like if this doctor truly knew how much detail I give these things I might end up in a straightjacket.

"Interesting. That's a nice story. What about before her? Who else did you think about last night?"

I give her the barebones account of Gregory with the dogs and Calla the waitress. She chuckles at Groomer Has it but otherwise stays silent and motionless. I tell her about Jimmy the goat head warrior and that leads to the anxiety attack I felt after.

She's easy to talk to. It all spills out. I want to get better and she needs to know if she's going to help me.

She asks questions or for clarification here and there but mostly I just let it all out. I tell her about my stories getting me in trouble at work and how distracted I was while DJ was driving. I want her to know it's affecting my daily life. She occasionally looks at her clock or jots something down but listens intensely. Something on her desk buzzes and we both look at it. Has it been an hour already?

"Nancy, I need you to know you're safe. I need you to take a deep breath and know that everything is going to be okay." I bolt out of my seat. This can't be good. We must have gone over our time or something is wrong. She also gets up but encourages me to sit. She brings a smaller chair next to mine.

"Nancy, I've asked your husband to join us. I'm going to open the door and let him in now. I promise you everything is okay." I start breathing fast and swallow hard. My face feels hot.

"You called my husband?!" I am outraged. "This can't be legal, this is unprofessional." I cry out as she reaches the door. I spring up again to meet him.

Daniel walks in, obviously as freaked out as I am. He shakes Dr. Harris's hand and takes me into an embrace. "Nance, baby, I had no idea." He murmurs into my neck. No idea about what? Did this woman tell on me? Did she tattle to my husband about skipping work and mind trips? I turn to her, about to give her a piece of my mind when Danny gently guides me back to the chairs where she is seated. He takes my hand and holds it tightly and looks over to the doctor.

"What the heck is going on?" I throw out, directing it to both of them.

"Nancy, you said some things that were inconsistent with the information in your chart. As we spoke, I realized that you're living in a delusional state. I apologize, I lied when I left to call my son's school, I needed to talk to your husband."

"I dropped everything and came right over." Daniel added. "I mean, of course I did. This actually makes a lot of sense. We'd thought it was just normal, given…" He trails off. "What happened. Everyone was stunned and hurt. Are you sure, Dr. Harris?"

"Why are you talking to her, baby?" I plead. "It's me. You know I'm okay. I don't know what she told you, I don't have any idea what she's talking about. I day dream. It's not that big of a deal."

"Nancy, when was the last time you talked to Patrick?" Dr. Harris is still cold and even.

"What does that have to do with anything?" I am so confused.

"You mentioned last night, you two danced in the kitchen?" She waits for me to confirm.

"Yes. That's normal. Just a normal thing for a mother and son. I wanted to see if I liked a new band. Is this really that big of a deal?!" I can't fathom why Danny and Dr. Harris are asking about this.

Danny looks to Dr. Harris and she nods. He kisses my hand and softly says, "Babe, that's not possible." I make a face of disbelief at him.

"It was just a silly moment before dinner, Danny. Why are you guys making such a fuss?"

"Nancy, Patrick is gone. You know that, right?"

"What do you mean, gone? Danny, what is going on?!" I'm frantic now. Are they going to tell me something happened to my son? No, that doesn't make sense. He's fine. He woke up early and walked to school this morning. He goes to Foothills Middle School. He's a soccer player and has a bright red head of hair and a big, goofy smile.

"Nancy, Nance, Patty died two summers ago." Daniel exhales in pain. "You have to remember that, don't you? At soccer camp? Baby," He kisses my hand again, starting to break with emotion. "Babe, Patty is gone."

My brain suddenly remembers dropping my phone and screaming, frantically driving like a maniac to Cheney, the emergency room doctor saying they did everything they could. I remember picking up the little plastic box at the funeral home and sprinkling ashes on the soccer field. I remember people bringing casseroles and flowers. But that wasn't us. I made that up. That was someone else.

Wasn't it?

I scream as it comes back to me. My son, my perfect baby boy, is dead. Danny blurs as my eyes fill with tears before everything goes dark.

***

I wake, but I'm not in my bed. There's a machine beside me. I've got an IV in my arm. My wrists are cuffed to the side rails. I'm not wearing my clothes. I go to speak, to yell, to ask for help but darkness envelops me and I go back to sleep.

***

I dream about Dr. Harris and Danny making it all up to hospitalize me and start their lives together. They met at a conference and hit it off because they both work out and like the Seattle Seahawks. Once they have me declared incompetent, they can marry and she can legally adopt my sons.

My son.

I only have one son.

I don't want to wake up.

***

"Nancy? Nancy, can you hear me?" I see light and hear a male voice and feel something on my face. They're waking me up. I am still in a hospital bed but no longer cuffed and my IV is removed. I am sore everywhere. My throat is on fire and my mouth is dry.

"I can hear you. Can I have some water?" I croak. I see a man in a white coat. He's in his 40s, bearded balding. He nods to an aide or a nurse as his side and she pours me a cup. He adjusts the bed to sit me up.

"How do you feel?" He asks.

"Sore. Okay. How long was I asleep?" I answer after I take a sip. I realize I have a massive headache and mention that too.

"You've been medicated for about 30 hours now. The headache is normal, but we'll give you some pain medication if you'd like. You were on haloperidol but we've weaned you off. We've also been giving you lithium and you may continue to feel groggy or sleepy. Over the next few days, we will figure out what medications and doses are right for you. Do you understand?"

I feel like it doesn't matter if I object. I nod.

"Do you know what year it is?" He asks.

"It's October 15th or 16th of 2018." I answer. I'm unsure what 30 hours plus Thursday is and my head is now pounding.

"How many fingers am I holding up?" I see three and I tell him so.

"Great, great. Ok, who lives in your house with you?"

"My husband and my son, DJ. I know Patrick is dead. I was

just confused, I'm not crazy." I don't want to appear argumentative, but I also think this all got out of hand.

"It's ok, Nancy. What you went through, I can't imagine." He is softer now. "We're just here to help."

"Can I see my husband?" I ask. I need to make sure he isn't mad, isn't going to take Danny Jr. away from me.

"Likely not today, but soon. I'm sure he's eager to see you too. We will call him and let him know you're awake and doing well." He looks at my chart. "You just missed breakfast. Are you hungry? I can snag something for you from the vending machine."

"No, I'm not hungry. Just the headache. Can I walk around?" I try to peek out the little window in my door.

"Yes, but let's keep it to this room for now and only when an aide or a nurse is around."

He helps me out of the bed and the aide escorts me to the restroom. It doesn't have a door. This isn't a standard hospital room. I can't have privacy because I'm the sad, lunatic mom who imagined her son was still alive.

***

I meet with my coordinated care counselor later that afternoon. She will be my primary therapist while I'm here and transitioning back home. She's hopeful it will only be another day here and a few weeks to tweak the medications. During that time, I will meet with her three times a week and formulate a plan.

I quietly agree to it all, again, certain I don't have a choice. Her name is Christina Farmer and insists I call her Chrissy. She's about my age and has tight, bouncy curls.

I feel weird. Woozy and sedated, certainly, but also numb. It feels like I should have bigger emotions; I should be anxious and scared and sad and freaking out but it is only a vacuous hole where my feelings usually sit. That's likely preferable, given that I just lost my son. Again.

***

Danny picks me up with a change of clothes. He's in hyper-focused, efficiency mode. I'm pleased to see he isn't upset with me. I don't know exactly why I thought he would be. It is strange that I basically pretended our son was alive for 27 months and he never really said anything. I will definitely talk to him about that later. He's getting prescription information from the charge nurse and trying to ask her if I can be alone without letting me know that's what he's asking. I'm curious too. I know I can be alone; I'm not going to hurt myself or anyone else.

She assures him I'm okay, but for the next few days I should have someone around, just in case. The charge nurse is blonde and pretty, tall and seems completely over it all. Maybe it's the end of a long shift, maybe she had to work a double, again. Her name is Lucy and she's dedicated to her work but sometimes wishes she'd gone into wedding planning like her sister. Lucy is, wait, I can't remember what's next. I lost my train of thought.

I am having trouble getting my pants on. I'm in the tiny bathroom, trying to have at least a little privacy and realized I tried to put the pant leg over my slipper. Lucy and Danny look over to me with pity. I don't blame them.

In the car, I tell Danny I don't want my sister to come. He assures me he hasn't told her anything other than I was briefly hospitalized for 'exhaustion' and she should steer clear. I actually wouldn't mind seeing Candy, I just couldn't handle her daughters right now. Or be able to look her in the face if she knew what I had done. I think back to all the times I told her I couldn't watch the girls because Patty had practice, all the times people just shrugged and assumed I was grieving or misspeaking. All the times the coach sadly thanked me for the snacks and no other parents sat near me.

A tear falls down my cheek but I don't feel sad.

I ask what he told DJ. He hems and haws and confesses that he told the boy everything. I guess they had to compare notes on Mom's crazy behavior and how they missed it. As if reading my mind, Danny takes my hand as he pulls into the pharmacy. He looks at me earnestly and apologizes.

"I could say I had no idea. I mean, I didn't really know, but I just thought it was how you grieved." He kisses my hand again. "Everything else was normal, and it was kinda sweet how you'd set out four plates or go see his team play. I'm so," His voice cracks, "I am so, so sorry."

I try to remember those moments, setting out a plate for Patty-Cake, but it's all fuzzy.

I pull his hand up to kiss him back. "Are we okay?" I ask. Another involuntary tear falls down my face.

"We will be." He answers honestly. "Your doctors have a really good plan and we will be us again. I promise."

How can we be us if I don't even know who I am?

***

We pull into the garage and I hesitate. I worry my feet will be unsteady. I worry what our home's dynamic will feel like. Am I now the lunatic mother in the rocking chair being placated and handed cups of hot tea for my nerves? I hate tea. Will Daniel institutionalize me? The thoughts are worrisome, but I'm so medicated I don't have the visceral reaction I should. I slid gently out of Danny's SUV with his help and we walked arm-in-arm into the house, the same walk we took after we said 'I do'. We are certainly testing our vows. He agreed to sickness, but was there a whack-a-do clause?

He's being so cautiously doting. I've never more strongly wished for my gift of imagining another's thoughts more in my life. It seems to be gone, drugged to oblivion. I could ask. I'm afraid of the answer.

I rarely ask people how they feel, now that I think about it. I just assume I know and work off that information. I wonder if that's why I don't have any close friends. I used to. Shari in high school and then Brigit, Bri - I called her. Bri and I met in Lamaze class when I was pregnant with DJ. We were the same age, the youngest in the class. Our husbands were both busy in school, Daniel of course at Chiropractic School and her husband, Mike, studying to be an engineer. We bonded instantly and were grateful for the mutual support.

Bri is a dainty, tiny thing with white blond hair and delicate features. She's always talking, babbling, and flitting about. I loved how I never had to wonder what Bri was thinking - she never left a thought unsaid. I can see where some would find that annoying. I love it. Well, I loved it.

I haven't had a real conversation with Bri since Patty died. I never took time to think about it until now, but I lost all my 'mom friends', who were my only friends. I've always been the kind to only have one close friend and few people I know well. I'm content with my own company. After I met Danny, I didn't need the companionship of others often. Bri is the kind of friend that doesn't wait for your invitation. She is the kind of person that simply shows up - often. Again, she was.

Bri would let herself in and set her son, Brandon, into DJ's play area and settle on the couch next to me and start talking as if we were already mid-conversation. She'd gossip about other moms or complain about the new coat she'd purchased on-line or sometimes just grab my hair and start playing with it, envious of the length and thickness. Bri's thin hair simply won't grow past her shoulders as if her endless energy vibrates it off.

We both found out we were pregnant with our second children a week apart. We went as far as to have our ultrasounds on the same day so neither of us had to wait. I was thrilled for her when she learned she was going to have a girl and happy to know I would have two sons so close in age. I would have been happy either way, but Brigit was eager to have a little girl to dress up in cute clothes. I had hoped our family would grow much more, ideally four children or even six if I was healthy enough. Danny's one of seven kids - Mormons, you know - and I delighted in the thought of our own little squadron of Caulkins. Bri was happy to finally have her daughter, Britney, and got an IUD. We would go on to constantly joke about Patrick and Britney growing up soulmates and eventually marrying.

Bri didn't work outside of the home. She was a sucker for pyramid schemes and sold makeup and skin care and weight loss teas. She was never pushy about it, not to me. When we last caught up, she was doing really well selling leggings and t-shirts in pop-up shops in people's homes. I liked this scheme the best, the leggings were incredibly comfortable and I enjoyed attending the little parties. Since she was free during the day, her kids in school, she would pop over to my office and we'd eat lunch together at the downtown fountain. Our friendship was effortless.

When she found out about Patrick, she rushed over and threw the door open and didn't bother to close it. She bee-lined for me and held me in an aggressive bear-hug, sobbing and wailing. She was gasping for air against my shoulder. I had already had my crying breakdown and was now numb. I stroked her thin hair and shushed her like a baby. When she finally settled and composed herself, she promised me that she would be there, whatever I needed. I couldn't think of anything to say other than, "You left the door open."

Brigit kept her word for the first week. She was often over at our home before I woke up, cleaning and scrubbing and dealing with all the visitors and casseroles. But something had changed in how she treated me, how she talked to me. She stopped sharing every thought, our collective contemplations too sorrowful and macabre to say out loud. She stopped looking at me as her dull but kind friend Nancy. I was now the embodiment of her worst fear. I was pitied and, eventually, avoided.

I don't blame her. Nor do I blame the other moms. I imagined they all went to bed at night, thanking every conceivable God above that it wasn't them. I imagine they all did mental gymnastics to justify how this could never happen to them, they would have done preliminary allergy tests on their children or assured the soccer camp would have an epi-pen at the ready at all times. They could imagine the pain of happily living your life, of loving your kids with all you have, only to have it all shattered with a phone call. And the imagery itself was so painful they had to look away from the woman who was living in their nightmare. Even if she was her closest friend.

***

Danny sets up a little camp for me on the couch, water and tissues and magazines and a crossword on a little table he has moved next to it. He's rearranged all the pillows and set up my favorite cozy blankets. I don't argue but I would much rather be in bed. Everything feels both heavy and too light. I'm also tired but it's far too early to sleep. I make a half-honest offer to make dinner but Danny announces he's ordered take out at my favorite Italian place. I like Risolli's for the ambiance and the loud, archaic owners yelling at each other from the kitchen. I love the tacky, red candle holders and the big wooden booths. The food isn't all that great or original. It's too late to change it and I'm not hungry anyway.

Danny is pacing around, obviously nervous about something. DJ is sitting at the dining room table, ruler-straight posture, doing his homework.

"Babe?" I inquire timidly. "What's the matter?"

"I need to pick up the food." He says. I look at him quizzically but I realize he's afraid to leave me alone.

"DJ is here." I offer. "I will be okay. I promise." His gaze oscillates from me to DJ and back, considering. I worry perhaps my son doesn't want to be alone with me or my husband is afraid of leaving me with him. How did all this happen so quickly? Just days ago, I was a trusted and reliable mom. However, I guess I wasn't. These two have the right to feel unsure about me. I motion to Danny to sit next to me. He acquiesces with minimal hesitation and I snuggle up on his shoulder.

"I can't imagine how you must feel right now. All of this is unthinkable. And you've been amazing." I rub my hand over his forearm and he relaxes into me a little more. "I hope I can rebuild your trust."

He interrupts. "Nancy, I trust you! Of course, I trust you."

I take his hand and tilt my head to get his gaze. I am exhausted but I try to keep it from showing on my face. "Ok, you trust me. You're worried. Me too." I take his hand and kiss it. "I will be alright for 20 minutes. If you don't want DJ to be alone with me or if maybe he doesn't, I will be okay."

He kisses my forehead and exhales into it. "I am so scared,

Nan. Not of you, but for you."

I start to tell him that I understand but DJ is now standing in front of us. "Dad," He starts, "Go get the food. Mom is fine and I'll be here. I want to." He pauses. "I want to be here." Danny gets up and DJ takes his place next to me. DJ is now two full inches taller than me, but I pull his torso up on my lap. I look up at Danny and mouth 'twenty minutes'. He gives me a half smile and heads out.

I have no idea what to say. My brain feels foggy and all thoughts are slippery; I can't hold them for more than a few seconds. DJ doesn't seem to mind. He's facing away from me and equally silent. We stay there, motionless, watching a TV screen playing some sitcom with volume so low we can barely hear it. Eventually, I'm too weak to keep my eyes open and I doze off in the unexpressed comfort.

***

I wake the next morning to Danny bringing me breakfast in bed. I'm groggy and confused, but touched by the sweet, although unnecessary, gesture. I start to ask him why I'm getting such luxurious treatment, but then remember. I lived in a delusional state for over a year. He brings over the pill box he'd already filled for me and realize I probably have to take these with food.

My husband can't stand the thought of me being unmedicated for even a few minutes.

He asks if he can get me anything. I tell him I need to use the restroom and would love a cup of coffee. He raises his eyebrows and I realize my husband doesn't know that I drink coffee. He doesn't like the smell so I always waited to make a cup after he left for the day or would have some at work where we always have a pot going.

I wonder what else Danny doesn't know about his wife of 17 years. From the look on his face I wonder if he's thinking the same thing.

***

After breakfast, I get myself ready for my first appointment with Chrissy, my primary counselor. Her title suggests I will have many. I start to feel a wave of anxiety. Will I ever be normal again? How long will it take for all of this to blow over? As quickly as it washes over me, it flees into the medicated void of my mind. I suppose normal wasn't really normal anyway.

I open my drawer to pick the right pair of pants. I want to feel comfortable, but I will not look unkempt. I refuse to give this woman ammunition against me. I see the ripped jeans I'd planned on wearing to that live music show with Danny. I was so looking forward to that. My eyes feel the urge to cry and face tenses, but nothing. Again, the medication doesn't allow me to wallow or sit with my regret. It's just numb, nothing, static.

I select a newer pair of leggings and pair them with a cute sweater and suede knee-high boots. It's comfortable but I look put together. I braid my still damp hair loosely and examine my face in the mirror, contemplating what makeup would mean to a therapist in this situation. If I wear makeup, would she think I'm still delusional, still pretending that everything is perfectly normal and status quo? If I don't wear it - am I depressed and need more medications?

Honestly, I need it. My skin is patchy and pale and I have dark bags under my eyes despite all the extra sleep a medication and trauma induced psychotic break allows. I decide to err on the side of vanity and use a little concealer, blush, and mascara. I don't wear much more than this most days.

I find Danny pacing by the door. He's eager for this appointment. It dawns on me that Wenatchee's busiest chiropractor is at home on a weekday. I ask him how he's missing work.

"I've cancelled everything, Nan. For at least this week. And Nathen Figaroa is coming up next week to fill in for me." He answers me as simply as if I'd asked the time.

This man couldn't find time to have lunch with me just two weeks ago. Danny hasn't taken two weeks off work since Patty-cake was born.

Or when he died. Or did he? I can't remember right now. He took some time off, certainly. My now-feeble brain tried to remember. We got back from Cheney late - it was dark out. He took the next day off; he was with me and DJ all day. Wasn't he? No, since Brigit was there, he told me he might as well go to work. "People are in pain." He had said. "I might as well go be productive."

He helps me into his car and gets behind the wheel. With the determined caution of a pilot, he pushes the garage opener and watches the door carefully, fully turned in his seat. He precisely backs out and pauses again, watching the door slowly lower. I am trying to remember if Danny had always been this vigilant or if this was more kid-glove treatment for his wife who lost her marbles.

At the end of our street, I see the meter maid, erm, well, meter-man. Most everyone on the block is read by binoculars or radio, but the old man on the corner has his meter on the back of his house and a locked gate. I'd talked to the meter-reader, yes, that's the term, about it before. What was his name? It's on the tip of my tongue, but I'm bad with names while this doped up. I wonder if he has kids. I wonder if he has a spouse. I wonder who he has lost.

I bet he lost a parent already. I have. That's an especially lonely club to join at 16 but we get new members all the time. That's what Shari and I called it: the Dead Moms Club. She joined as a baby, but it still hurt her constantly. Meter-Man is in the Dead Dad Club, though. Last year, cancer, it was rough, slow. Meter-Man lost his first and best friend.

Did he tell me this? No, we've barely spoken. This is my brain doing that thing. Just not as well as it usually does.

***

Chrissy's office is nowhere as sleek or professional I was expecting. I thought it would be like Dr. Harris's but it's cluttered and tiny, barely bigger than a cubicle. There's only room for her desk and a chair facing it and a plant. She welcomes me warmly and asks if I'd like something to drink.

Usually, I would decline, but I never did get a cup of coffee this morning. It felt awkward with Danny after I brought it up and I changed the subject. I asked her if that was possible. She visibly relaxed her body and exclaimed: "Oh my God, that sounds amazing!" She motions for me to follow her.

"The nurses' lounge always has a pot going and they have all the good creamers." She explains on the way. "Our break room has one of those stupid Keurigs, you know?" She doesn't wait for me to reply. "I can't get used to them. Plus, all that waste from the pods. I mean, I guess they have reusable pods but that seems like more of a hassle than a brew basket and a filter." She opens the door and I feel like when I was a kid and Mrs. Sorenson sent me to the teacher's lounge for her notebook - I am in the forbidden zone, granted a temporary pass but I must be quick and quiet. I look around for some sort of motivational poster, the classic kitten grasping to the screen with 'Hang in There' written over it. But this isn't an elementary school, these nurses have the modern classic: Live, Laugh, Love about their couch.

Whatever keeps you going, I guess.

"Nancy?" Chrissy was saying something. She hands me my mug and points to the coffee pot.

"Sorry, I think these meds make me a little spacy." It feels nice to have something to blame other than my own scrambled brain.

She tells me we'll discuss that further in her office and shows me the creamer selection. She was right, the nurses know what they're doing. I select a caramel mocha variety and take one last look around the lounge, still feeling like I'm somewhere I shouldn't be and will get caught any moment.

***

When we sit back down, Chrissy gets right to business. "You mentioned you're experiencing some side-effects to the medications? What did you take this morning and when?" She has a notepad ready. I tell her that Daniel gave them to me and I didn't read the bottles, but knowing him I was taking the exact doses as prescribed.

"I'm glad you have a solid support system." She pauses. "I have you scheduled for the same time for the next two days, morning appointments. I would like you to taper to a half dose of the lithium tomorrow morning and we'll see if we can take you off that completely." I contemplate what she intends with that.

"Don't I need to be medicated? I mean, I don't want to," I pause, "I can't do that again." I don't want to use the wrong words but I also don't want to put my family through any more hardship.

"Nancy, I will continue to meet with you regularly. We'll taper that down too, of course, but I will supervise you every step of the way. Your whole care team believes this was a serious delusional event brought on by, likely, PTSD. Looking at your records, possibly C-PTSD. You need help to process, but you probably don't need to be on antipsychotics."

I have many questions but start with: "I know what PTSD is, but I have never heard of C-PTSD. Also, I know what happened was terrible, but PTSD is like, war heroes and people who are," I paused and then whisper, "raped?" I continue lightly, "I don't, I don't think I have that."

"Post-Traumatic Stress Disorder can manifest after any trauma. Have you ever heard the phrase, 'You can drown in a bucket as fast as the ocean'?" I nod. I've heard some variation, I'm sure. She continues: "Mental health doesn't have the testing you would see in most other disorders. I can't look at your blood test and say, oh yes, she has this and we treat it with that. It's more complicated. Messy. But we do know what certain disorders look like and act like and we can say 'To the best of our powers of deduction you have this' and hope for the best. You had a very traumatic thing happen to you." She pauses to make sure I'm keeping up. "You had a mental reaction to the traumatic thing. That looks and acts like PTSD."

"Have you seen this before? Is this something that happens?"
I ask. "Do other mothers do this, you know, after, after,
something like that?" I hadn't even for a moment thought I
wasn't singular in this experience.

"Grief can present in many ways after a loss of this kind. You
are absolutely not alone." She pauses. "While I cannot tell you
how many people experienced it the exact way you did, this
specific delusion is not unheard of at all." The medicines block
the comfort and warmth I feel from her words. It's there but
lightly, like the flavor in seltzer.

***

Too soon after, she escorts me to the waiting area where
Danny is already in action mode - a notebook in his hand.
He's taken the time I was away to prepare questions for
Chrissy. I feel as though I should be embarrassed, but don't. I
look over to the man seated by the water cooler. Is he waiting
for his spouse too? He's got his legs crossed comfortably and
a complacent look on his face. Is he as medicated as me? I'm
barely functioning, as if I'm one moment away from drool
slipping out of the corner of my mouth. I compulsively wipe it.

The man is older than me, grey all over, not just his hair, a
grey sweater over dark grey slacks. He could be a teacher,
maybe, or, oh, what's that job, the one at the bank, not a teller,

above that. My fractured brain can't find the word. I wipe my mouth again.

"Nancy?" Danny gently taps my shoulder.

"Loan officer." I answer. No, that's not right either. Danny looks so confused. I am too.

***

While he drives us home, Danny asks me about my appointment. I answer his questions, holding nothing back. He seems displeased with what I have to say. My husband is analytical; he wants a clear timeline of when I will be healed. He murmurs something about gluten and I tune him out.

We pass the fountain downtown by my work and I suddenly remember that I have a job.

"Danny, did you call my work?" I ask.

"Yes." He pauses. "I told them that you're on medical leave and would contact them when you could. That boss of yours, Frankie? He's a real piece of work." I can tell Danny was censoring himself.

"What did he say?" I am curious but also a little afraid.

"Nance, I'm not sure if you'll want to go back to work anyway."
The finality of words let me know Frankie Jr. likely told my
husband I didn't have a job anymore. I don't think that's legal,
but I also couldn't care less.

And that's not just the meds.

***

Chrissy doesn't bother taking me to her office, we head
straight to the nurse's lounge from the waiting area. We get
our possibly illicit coffee and settle in. I report feeling more
lucid today, less tired and heavy. But with that comes an
unnerving anxiety, as if I've left the stove on or my gas cap off.
I have a constant ringing in my head that there's something
off, forgotten.

"Which is weird," I confess. "I didn't feel this way when I was,
you know, forgetting something really important in my life." I
still dance around the words. When I was delusional about my
son's death and pretended for over a year he was still an
alive, giggly boy.

Chrissy doesn't let me dance. "When you were delusional
after a massive loss." She takes a breath to let the words
settle between us. "I would like to talk about that a little today,

if you're comfortable." I nod, despite my uncertainty.

"Can you remember the shift? When you started seeing him again?" I shake my head. I've tried to think back to it, to relive those moments.

"No. I remember the week after, I remember Bri and Danny, both were frantically trying to distract themselves with errands and chores. I mostly sat on the couch. I was closer to my dad and sister then so they were over a lot. I remember the day DJ asked us if he could go back to school and we all decided to try to just go back to our normal lives. I went to work. I think it wasn't a drastic change, one day he was back. I don't really know." I look down and notice I'm wringing my hands forcefully; they're red. I let go and shake them out.

"OK, that's an assignment for you. I need you to ask Danny and the rest of your family when or if they noticed you started acting differently, especially the physical actions like setting out a plate of food or taking snacks to the soccer team. Who is Bri? You've not mentioned her."

"She was my friend. We used to be close. We stopped talking shortly after. She wouldn't know." I try to think back to the last time I spoke with her. I can't remember. I know she sent me a birthday card a couple months ago and I sent a thank you note.

"It could be helpful to reconnect with friends, Nancy. This process, getting you well, could be painful and you need all the support you can get." I consider her words and imagine that phone call. *'Hey, Bri, turns out I went completely coo-coo and my therapist says I need friends. Do you want to get lunch this week?'* I don't think I can do that.

As if reading my mind, Chrissy says, "It won't be easy. None of this will be easy. You want to get better, right?" I nod. "Listen, I know you probably think all of this was a much bigger deal than it is. It seems like an impossible situation that won't get better, right?" I nod again, I'm starting to feel lethargic. She continues: "I promise you; you can live a completely normal life. It won't look or feel like it did two years ago, that's impossible. But you are not broken. You suffered an unimaginable loss, a couple of them, and your brain chose to deal with them in an unhealthy way."

"A couple of them?" I inquire.

"This is speculation on my part, but from what we've discussed and what we understand of these things, this is why I'm thinking it's C-PTSD, or Complex Post Traumatic Stress Disorder." I remember now, I was going to look that up. "Your son wasn't your first trauma. Your mother died when you were thirteen, correct."

"Yes, but that was ages ago. I'm fine." I don't see what that has to do with anything. I dealt with it. It was awful, but I grieved her properly. I didn't imagine she was still around, picking up the house or braiding my hair.

"You also mentioned your father is an alcoholic?" I nod, she continues. "Did your mother also drink?"

"Yes." I am sensitive about that. Mom's drinking was quieter than Dad's, but still in every memory of my childhood.

"Nancy, your parents gave you no modeling of healthy coping mechanisms. How did your dad react to your mother's death?"

"He drank more." I answer simply.

"And how did you cope?" I think about her question for a moment.

"I just took care of my little sister and the house the way Mom would have wanted me to. I don't know. I was young. I didn't know about these things." Blood rushes into my face. "I just tried really hard to forget. I was busy taking care of things and school and stuff."

"I'm not shaming you, Nancy. No one really knows how to properly grieve. We do know that if you don't process that grief, it can manifest into unhealthy behaviors. Like drinking."

"I don't drink!" I interrupt.

"I know. You are very responsible. You've done incredibly well, considering how most people would survive these things." Her voice is calming. I did get defensive. "I was saying, they can manifest in various ways: drinking or drugs are common. Or sleeping around, or eating disorders, or sometimes, just sometimes, when you experience another crushing loss, you have a mental break."

It clicks. I didn't know how to lose my son. So, I didn't.

"What will keep this from happening again?" I'm earnest. I drank her Kool-Aid. I am in, let's just fix this. I have C-PTSD and now we cure it.

She smiles. "Exactly what we're doing. We find the right meds and you continue therapy and over time, you will live a functioning, productive life."

I mull her words over in my head. Interesting that she didn't say happy, though. However, a part of me is comforted that she didn't over-sell it. Happiness is never guaranteed.

***

I leave Chrissy's office exhausted but have another appointment right after with Dr. Adkinson. He's my prescribing physician and I am told I've met him before and will see him whenever Chrissy suggests we make any major medication changes or if I have any adverse reactions. When he greets me, I know he looks familiar. He has grey, balding hair and a beard.

"How are you feeling today?" He starts.

"Anxious. I was telling Chrissy I feel like I'm forgetting something. Otherwise, okay. The lithium makes me tired and froggy."

"Froggy?" He looks at me inquisitively.

"You were there, when I woke up." I blurt. He asked me what day it was and how many fingers he was holding. I remember him now.

He laughs. "Yes, I was. I've been on your case since you were admitted."

"I meant foggy. See, it's like the car starts and runs, but not well. And sometimes misfires."

"That's an excellent analogy." He looks at his computer. "I'm looking at Chrissy Farmer's notes. You're lucky to have her, you know. She is excellent." I agree. "You're also lucky that you live here and have excellent health insurance. There are people with conditions like yours that wait years to find this kind of care. We started this cooperative approach, this focus on whole-person mental health only months ago. We got a grant from the University of Washington." He continues reading.

"Go Huskies." I don't know what else to say. I wouldn't have considered myself lucky to be in this situation, really. Regardless of grants and cooperation.

"I'm glad to see you have your humor." He chuckles. "I agree with Chrissy. Starting tomorrow, no more lithium. You had a good reaction to Celexa in the past?" I nod. I want to argue that I'm not depressed, but I am not sure.

"Let's start with 20mgs of that daily and 1 to 2mgs of Xanax as needed. Start that today, but it can take weeks to feel the effects of the SSRI. Take 1mg of the Xanax tomorrow morning instead of the lithium." He goes on to tell me the potential side effects and when I should call and report them. I nod, knowing he'll have to repeat every bit of this to Danny who will follow the directions exactly. I know I should feel comforted by Danny's care and concern, but there's something about it I don't like.

It comes back to him being unavailable for lunch. It took a mental breakdown to get his attention.

"Okay." Dr. Adkinson says with finality. "Any questions?"

I have hundreds. But nothing seems to come to mind and I thank him for his time.

Chapter 6:

"Babe, I swear I am okay. I can cook. I can do the laundry. I can drive. Dr. Adkinson and Chrissy both assured you I am completely fine to be alone while you're at work." This is the third time Danny and I have had this discussion.

"Maybe," I start, wrapping my arms around his shoulders and purring into his neck, "You can home for lunch and a little quickie." I've been throwing myself at my husband all this week. Ever since I heard the possible side effects of the antidepressant, I've forced myself to be as sexual as possible. I can't lose this part of my relationship with my husband. He's been mostly receptive to my advances, but far more gentle than usual. It's like he thinks he can break my brain again with the power of his penis.

He kisses my cheek and chuckles. "What has gotten into you?" He suddenly tenses.

"Nancy, is this an attempt to perhaps make another child? Are you trying to get pregnant again?" He's so serious; he sounds almost stern and accusatory.

"No!" I try to control my face and tone. "I just, I can't believe I have to say this out loud, I just want my husband and I want to feel close to him and I want us to be okay again. My IUD is still very much in place. We agreed: no more kids ages ago, when Patty was..." I trail away.

When Patrick was a baby and we miscarried. I never say those words out loud because I was so ashamed of the relief I felt to know I wasn't going to carry another child. I had just recovered from my postpartum depression; I was just fitting into my jeans again; I was just feeling good and whole again and back to work and Patty was sleeping through the night and I felt a light at the end of the tunnel and then I missed a period and my breasts were heavy and I just knew. And I was miserable.

I had wanted more children, but not so soon. Danny was elated, maybe a girl this time, or a pack of boys, he didn't care. He didn't have to carry the baby. He didn't have to breastfeed it. He didn't have to get up every two hours while also potty training another kid and cooking and cleaning. He was thinking of names and looking at minivans and I was dry-heaving and constantly crying.

We held each other tightly after I left the ObGyn's office. He wept against my chest and I felt a relief I could never, ever share with him or anyone or even myself. I told Danny the loss was too hard on me and I didn't want to get pregnant again. I got the IUD soon after and we settled on our family of two sons.

And then became a family with one. And then mom lost her mind.

I am so focused on my pain and suffering; I forget that salt-of-the-Earth Daniel has lost all this too. I wonder what his coping mechanisms are? Working too much, certainly. Does he cheat? Does he secretly gamble? In all this conflict and drama, my secrets are all coming out. What does my husband keep from me?

***

"Chrissy?" I sip my coffee and carefully plan the words I want to say. "Can the medications I'm on cause paranoia?"

"Do you think the toaster is listening to you?" She is casual with me pretty much always now. I appreciate it. There's an ease in our conversations. I fully trust her.

I laugh. "No!" I take a short breath. "Yesterday, for the first time ever in my marriage, I wondered if my husband is cheating on me."

"Whoa, ever?" She seems incredulous. "You've never once questioned his loyalty?"

"He's given me no reason. He's a very, very good man. He was raised Mormon, doesn't drink: a real family man."

"Mormons cheat. Family men cheat. Every kind of person is capable of cheating. Why did you suddenly question his fidelity?" She readies her pen, so I know my answer to this is important.

"With everything I kept from him, all my secrets, I have to wonder if maybe he has some too." I watch to see how much she writes down. Instead, she looks up at me, slightly confused.

"Did you have secrets?" She asks.

"I... I..." I fumble on the words. "I pretended our dead son was still alive?" Now I'm confused.

"Nancy." She seems slightly exasperated. "You weren't consciously keeping that from him. This wasn't a lie, there was no deceit." She pauses. "You didn't know, you were delusional. It would be normal to blame yourself a little, but it's extreme to call it a secret or pretending. Did he imply that he felt deceived?"

"No." That's the truth. Danny has been nothing but supportive and positive.

"Did you have other secrets?" She asks carefully.

I pause. "I kept the day-dreaming from him. I kept that from everyone. I can't stress how often or out-of-control it was." I pause again. I momentarily weigh my trust in this woman I barely know. "I never told him why I didn't want more kids after Patty, at least, never the whole truth." That's a lot easier to say than: 'I'm glad I miscarried'.

"He doesn't get a say in your reproductive choices, Nancy. He can express his desires, but at the end of the day it was your body and future." She is firm. I can tell she's pro-choice, but I would have guessed that before we spoke a word to each other. Her tiny nose stud and the way she dresses - it's clear she's liberal.

I bet she went to Western or Evergreen. All the super liberal girls from high school ended up at one of those two schools, well, the ones that went to college. Chrissy probably went to

Western. Which means she lived in Bellingham for years. I wonder how she ended up in Wenatchee.

Christina Lyn Farmer was the youngest daughter of Jerry Farmer in Richland, Washington. Her mother left the family shortly after her birth, choosing drugs and wild men over their three beautiful girls. Chrissy's older sisters are twins and ended up much like their mother, fond of adventures and risky choices with their bodies and hearts. Chrissy was a fat child, desperate to please and be liked. She wanted nothing more than her father's approval for who she was, not how she wasn't her sisters. She ate to cope with everyone's constant arguing and shouting.

She found a Richard Simmons book at the library when she was in 10th grade and it changed her life. She got a perm and lost 80 pounds. She would reconnect with her mother the next year and spend a summer with her. Chrissy came back different: with a steeled determination to fix in others what was so broken in her mother. She started looking into Psychology programs and that's what got her to Western Washington University in Bellingham.

How she got to Wenatchee also goes back to her mother.

"Nancy? Nancy?" Chrissy is waving at me, concerned.

Oh no. Oh no, no, no.

***

"How was your appointment, babe?" Daniel asks as his lips brush my cheek. He just burst into the kitchen from the side door, vigorously. He smells like he went to the gym. I will never understand how he seems to be energized by working out. I tried cardio and yoga and swimming, nothing ever made me feel anything other than fatigued.

"Great." I lied. "Chrissy says I'm doing really well." That's not a lie. She did say that. She also didn't know all the information. She didn't know that I'd drifted off and daydreamed about her. Or that I was lying about being relieved that I miscarried. Or that I worry constantly that Daniel is going to leave me.

"That smells good." He points at the pan I'm currently stirring, a stir fry with shrimp and snow peas. I am enjoying the time off work to make meals I want to eat and not just what I can have ready in 20 minutes.

"Yeah?" I beam. "Try the sauce, I was thinking of adding some lemongrass paste. Would it be too much?" Daniel loves Asian foods. I knew this would make him happy.

"Oh, let's be daring, darling!" He squeezes the paste without caution into the pan and winks.

"Oh my!" I exaggeratedly gasp. "What will the neighbors think?" I turn around and press into the warm stove. I give him playful eyes and bring my hand up to clutch imaginary pearls.

"Screw 'em." Danny says with an eyebrow up as he wraps his arm around me and pulls me in for a deep, passionate kiss.

It all slips away in that moment. I'm not crazy. I'm not a bad person. My husband loves me. Life is wonderful and perfect.

***

I huff and puff and groan as I lose the battle with my refrigerator. I have two things on my To-Do list today: clean the kitchen and contact Bri. I'm procrastinating on the latter by pulling my appliances out and cleaning under them. I slip to the floor and contemplate my next move.

I don't even know how to start a conversation with my old best friend. Do I call her? Text? It's so awkward.

I remember all the beautiful stationary I have sitting unused in my desk and surrender victory to the stainless-steel Frigidaire.

I spend too long choosing the right paper and pen. I settled on a pretty ivory set with daisies embossed crisply along the edges. I chose my favorite gel pen in blue. I consider pencil, as I'm likely going to make several mistakes, but relish the idea of prolonging this task.

Dear Bri. No. *Dearest.* God no. *Hey Bri.* Yuck. *Hello.* I don't hate it.

Hello. Should I add Friend? *Hello Friend.*

I like that.

Hello Friend.

Found myself thinking about you today when I saw the crayon markings under my kitchen island that your little Brandon left when he was four or five years old. I still haven't attempted to clean them. How have you been? I've been well, especially since they lowered my lithium.

No.

Hello Friend.
Been awhile, hasn't it? This pretty paper made me think of you and inspired me to drop a line.

What could I possibly say next. I'm going to speak from the heart.

I miss your laugh, so loud it would sometimes hurt my ears and I miss the way you'd flap your hands when you were excited or angry. I miss how you'd sing hellooooo, knock, knock after you were already in my house. I miss having a friend in general but mostly I miss you.

Wow. I didn't know I felt this way. I can't send this but it's really good to know that about myself. I fold the paper in half and tuck it into my notebook. I pull out my phone and text: *Hey lady. Been a while. Want to get a coffee?*

Deep breath. Send.

***

The man walked toward me with a labored gait. His pants snug under a large belly and his suspenders demonstrating they are the hardest working device in the whole city of Wenatchee. He's got a flannel shirt testing the tensile strength of his buttons' thread as well. He's got a neatly trimmed long grey beard and one of those hats that only old men can wear.

He's so curious to see downtown. Certainly, he isn't headed here to the indie coffee roaster with unfinished brick walls and semi-obscene art. Or to the Yoga Cafe next door. Would he like the Boba place? I can't imagine it's the bespoke mountain bike shop or the Doggy Day Spa...well, maybe. Maybe he's one of those older men that spends his silver years doting on a Pomeranian.

He surprises me and takes a sharp left into Boba Place. I smile to myself at the thought of an older man sucking up those little jelly balls through a fat, pink straw.

I bet he does have a little dog too. Named Baby or Booger, depending on gender. A yappy, chubby, tiny thing that he would die for. His son got him the dog after his wife died. It was his fourth wife, but the one he'd decided to grow old with and she broke the contract with the terrible combination of diabetes and a sweet tooth. She was the one that got ol' George hooked on boba.

In his younger years, George was a logger but the profession made his wife dysfunctionally nervous and was hard on his back. He quit, but not in time to save his marriage with Frankie. He would acquire his second wife, Colleen, and his CDL the next year. Colleen is the mother of his children: the son who got him the dog and he sees twice a year and a daughter that was born with cystic fibrosis that never talked, walked, or had any real quality of life before dying at four-years-old. His marriage died with the little girl and started a rift with his son that never quite healed.

Wife number three ended up being a scam that broke poor George's heart and bank account. The woman was thoughtful and kind and loving until she had the ring and then made a complete shift. He would later learn he was her 7th husband and all had the same or similar stories. She was after their money. She preyed on older men who were comfortable but not rich enough to worry they could be a target. She would torment poor George day and night with outrageously loud music and wild parties and vicious words. It cost him every penny he'd ever saved and a loan against his house to rid of her.

George was happily celibate for nearly two decades after that debacle. He settled into a lonely but safe life. He would treat himself to a drink or two at the Eagles a few times a week, especially on cribbage Thursdays. He had many friendly acquaintances at the bar, but never let anyone too close. Hattie Jones basically had to hit him with a crib board to understand that she was interested. He resisted for some time, but when he saw her at the Spaghetti Night with Earl Browning, his fear of missing out won and he asked her out on a date. It took two more years for her to convince him to get married and sadly, she was gone as many years later.

I break from the contemplation and evaluate if this is healthy. This is the clearest I've been mentally since my hospitalization, well, likely in years, but also, this kind of fantasy can't be healthy. I made a note in my phone to bring it up with Chrissy and check the time.

Bri was never a timely person. We'd agreed to meet at 10:00AM and I knew that probably meant I'd see her at 10:20. I felt the anxiety rise up my chest and I took a deep breath. I tried to repeat Chrissy's words:

Connection is critical to my health. I need a support system.

I open my eyes and see her almost running toward me, a whirl of blond energy waving with both hands. I rose, without even thinking, to hug her. Her tiny body collided with mine and I was reminded of her unexpected strength and power. I felt as if she might lift me off the ground.

We separate and sit, grinning at each other. She delicately wipes her eye and I realize I've formed the beginning of tears too.

"It's so dang good to see you!" She beams. I repeat the sentiment. "How are you?" She continues.

"I'm...okay." I start. I take a deep breath. "I want to start with an apology though. I should have reached out much sooner." I'd taken careful analysis of our last regular communications on my phone. She'd invited me to her leggings parties and casino night at her kids' school. I didn't even reply.

"Ohmygawd, Nan!" She interrupted, "You have absolutely nothing to apologize for! In fact, it's me...Well, anyway, I'm just glad you reached out." She seemed to genuinely mean what she was saying.

Taking another deep breath, I continue: "I had some scary stuff happen with my mental health. My therapist said I need a bigger support system and encouraged me to rebuild our friendship. I know that sounds like an awful reason to call on you. Like, that's so crappy to only talk when I need something."

She interrupts again. "Nan, mental health...did you," She pauses looking for the right words. "Try to..." She trails off but I know where it was headed.

"Kill myself?" I ask. She nods, her eyes wide in horror. I realize it's weird that I never thought about that. I guess I knew how much DJ needed me. "No. I'll tell you more details later, it's honestly kind of embarrassing and a long story. But it did make me realize I was lonely."

She takes my hand in hers, visibly relieved and renewed with vim, "Not anymore. Now let's go to the counter and get giant coffees and you can tell me everything I missed. I mean ev-re-thing." She tightly grasps my hand and leads me toward the counter. I'm comforted by her leadership and take-charge attitude. I'm safe.

***

Feeling recharged by my lovely meet up with Bri, I decide to look over my homework from Chrissy. I will see her tomorrow and would love to present a completed list. I giggle a little at the idea of getting a gold star from my therapist. The next thing on the list is on-going, my medication journal. I'm to list what I took and when and check in on how I'm feeling every few hours, down to side effects like dry mouth or irritation and even deeply personal stuff like sex drive and constipation. I'd noted my morning doses and, ahem, deposits and note a noon check in of feeling great.

I do feel great. I haven't had this kind of freedom in a long time. It's been go-go-go with work and kids and…

Kid, Nancy. You have one kid.

The reminder stings briefly. I close my mental health notebook and add something of my own to the list. I want to see Patty's grave.

I cannot for the life of me remember anything about it. In all this time, all this delusion, had anyone visited? A good mother would make sure it was kept nicely and regularly had fresh flowers. I make a plan to get some daisies and head to the cemetery. I know which one it is, Wenatchee only has a couple and of course we chose one close to our house.

I hit the public market downtown for flowers. I could get them cheaper at a grocery store but I wanted to walk a little to see what's new. I stop by the local butcher's for some of his in-house apple-rosemary-chicken sausages and stock up on some vegetables from the grower's co-op. I should shop here more often. The flower selection was limited but I see some lovely white carnations that remind me of wedding bouquet. I don't know what the proper flowers are for this occasion, I'm sure there's a specific remembrance rose or something, but I like the frilly, lacey edge of the carnations.

After I've dawdled long enough at the open-air market, I make my way to the graveyard all too quickly. I'm piano wire tight and gripping the steering wheel so forcefully my knuckles are white. I was hoping it would come back to me when I got here, a mother's instinct, something. I have no idea where my son is. I park and start looking in the far left corner, making a plan to loop back to my van.

I remember his headstone was two or three feet tall so I don't bother checking any that are level to the earth. I walk carefully around, holding the flowers protectively to my chest. After a while, I noticed I was reading the names out loud.

Henry James Kindler, Maria Marisol Delgato-Sondoval, Catherine Dawn Grace.

Oh no, I knew her. I went to school with her. Oh, that's a shame. I had no idea.

I make a silent prayer for her and move on. Helen Ida Shipley. Major Mervin 'Merv' John Bussart. Thank you for your service, Merv. Guadalupe Isabelle Sanchez and Juan Carlos Sanchez. He died one year after she did. I read somewhere that's common: older men cannot survive after losing their wives. They either die or remarry quickly. I'm shocked my father is still around. Then again, he's self-embalming in whiskey.

Kerry Anne Fisher. I pause. She was young too. 1981-2002. After some quick mental math, she died at 21-years-old. Was it an accident? Capricious youth suffering the worst of consequences?

Kerry Anne was a popular girl that everyone liked. She had blonde, bouncy curls and a big smile. Her mom raised her on her own and put every ounce of energy into her only child. She waitressed at the little diner early mornings and lunch shift so she could be there for homework and dance classes. Her mom, Jennifer, never purchased anything nice or new for herself, always scrimping and cutting coupons to make sure she could provide for Kerry Anne.

It paid off when Kerry Anne got a huge grant to go to UCLA for dance performance and theatre. The two celebrated with ice cream sundaes and David Bowie. It was hard for Jennifer to watch her daughter move two states away, to move away from the tiny Valley that was all she ever knew to such a large city, but she never let her daughter see anything other than excitement and pride.

Kerry Anne excelled in school, mastering her craft and getting to perform in grand productions. Jennifer would save and visit once a year and Kerry came home for summers. After she graduated and got her first, real job working for a major studio, Kerry Anne flew home for Christmas to surprise her mom. The flight from Seattle to Wenatchee was canceled but that didn't stop the young woman, she rented a car and drove the three hours.

Well, she intended to. She hit some black ice on Blewett Pass and met her tragic end, head-on, with a logging truck.

Jennifer visits often, there's fresh flowers and the grass is well-manicured save a person sized divot right in front where she sits and talk to her daughter about what was, what is, and what could have been.

I wipe a tear from my eye and keep looking.

***

I remember the place just as I see it. I wore a long black dress that I threw away and Danny wore a soccer jersey from the team he and Patty loved and all the faces were blurred. Some of his ashes were buried here and then later we all spread the rest at the field. There were bright yellow flowers and simple guitar music flowed in the air. It was late summer, not too hot, pleasant breeze, and I remember hearing crickets as my father fell to his knees demanding God take him instead. My sister put her hand on my shoulder and told me that Patty was in heaven with Mom now and that was nice.

I wanted to punch her.

It's a crime against every bit of the humanity we have left to bury your child. I sit gently in front of his tombstone and weep.

I was hoping to feel him here. I haven't felt him since I 'woke up' from my delusion. I place my palm against his name and there's a spark of connection. It's not him, not even close, but it's all I have.

"I really miss you, baby." I say out loud in case there's some metaphysical realm where he can hear me but not read my mind. "You would be 12-years-old now. You'd be in 6th grade and finally at the Middle School by the house. I remember how eager you were to go there when DJ started. You couldn't wait to…"

He couldn't wait to grow up. The weight of the words and the grotesque irony silences me.

I catch my breath. "If you've got some sort of angel status, can you look after your brother. He's so quiet, I never know what's going on. Not like you: you rarely left a thought unexpressed." I chuckle. "He's going to be driving soon and I'm so, so worried. Look after your Aunt Candy too, she's still a train wreck. Although," I laugh again. "I guess I gave her some competition for family Nut Job, didn't I kid?"

"Were you there at all? Did you know what was going on? Was that confusing? I didn't mean to scare you - or anyone else. I think it was the only way I could survive losing you. I can't imagine a world where I just wake up and accept you're gone."

But I can. I've done it for weeks now. Heavily medicated, but I still wake up and accept the atrocious reality. Somehow.

"But I'm okay now. I have great doctors and your dad and I'm really going to be okay." And you'll still be gone. I can't stop crying. I'm freezing and my hands are turning blue, I need to leave soon.
"I love you baby, if you're somehow around and can hear me. I love you and miss you every day."

Out of nowhere, I felt warmed. The wind had stopped but also it felt like I was being hugged. I feel the pressure of invisible arms around me. I don't care if it's my imagination, I don't care if I get the straightjacket for this. I came here to feel my son and that's what I got. I no longer feel cold. I no longer feel sad or guilt or shame. Just love and warmth.

Chapter 7:

"You really think it was him?" Bri asks incredulously.

"I know I sound crazy. I know I AM crazy." I gesticulate toward my brain. She giggles. "But, yeah, I think his energy was there because I needed it. One last gift from my son."

Bri pops a plump, red grape in her mouth and half-garbles: "That's beautiful."

I inhale deeply and smile and nod. I also check the clock, worriedly. I know Danny won't be home for hours, but deceit makes you paranoid.

I don't know why I am keeping my revived friendship with Brigit from my husband. I think part of me likes having a little privacy right now, with Daniel meticulously tracking my medications and therapy appointments. He's come home and inquired about my bowel movements before even bothering to greet me. I don't always feel like his wife or a person; I am a patient.

Also, he's been fairly critical of my choices since the breakdown. I understand why - I do - but the other day when I went to the cemetery and came home so excited and filled with peace, he was instantly disapproving and almost angry I hadn't consulted him first.

I will tell him about Bri, soon. I don't like how this feels. It's dishonest, if only by omission.

"What's on your mind Birdie?" Bri had started calling me that recently. It's for Coo-coo bird, but I know it's meant with love. I'm thrilled to have any nickname other than Nan. Or worse: Nanny. I like when Danny calls me Nance. I've never had a nickname before. Birdie is cute. Birdie is cool. Bri and Birdie conquer the world! "Oh, not much." I lie. "The meds can make me a little spacy." She nods.

"Well, you wanna fly the coupe?" She grins at her own wit and puts the grapes back in my fridge. "We can go shopping." She faces me and lifts an eyebrow.

Bri lives for Target. It's not an errand for her, it's a hobby. Although I don't enjoy the mindless consumerism the way she does, I quickly agree to go.

I can feel the change in Bri's energy when we arrive. She's suddenly a child at a birthday party, she's a puppy at the park. I feel a chromatic buzz from two feet away.

I can't imagine something so simple making her so happy. Where does she get her joie de vivre? She's always invested in the moment, so present, but also light and gay and free. How could I learn this? Probably less likely with these medications.

She buzzes straight to the dollar section in the front making me sniff some candles and losing it over some llama tchotchke. She hadn't gotten a cart yet and already chose two items to buy. I get one for us so I can set my handbag down.

***

"It really doesn't matter, Nance." Danny assured with a finality that suggested he was done with the topic. I'd inquired into our finances without my income. I know I had medical expenses too. Danny's practice does well but we're not wealthy. I suppose it was also a little guilt at the impulse shopping I'd done with Bri today. I spent a couple hundred dollars on a few updates to my wardrobe. I really like what's in style these days and the shoes were so cute and before I knew it, the cart was full.

I didn't tell Danny but I also didn't lie about it. I just didn't mention it. And hid the bags.

I warm lotion in my hands and motion for him to take his shirt off. He does and I take a brief moment to appreciate the lean muscle. He's got a great body. I use a delicate hand and make sure I get every inch. I want him to feel how much I love him through my hands, the way I felt Patty at the cemetery. This whole thing has got me thinking about afterlives and heaven and souls. I was raised to believe there's a God in heaven and most of us get to go meet him when we die. My parents weren't super religious, we attended a mild, polite Lutheran service on Easter Sundays and occasionally when mom was cornered by an aunt or other distant relative. We never went again after she died; Dad's salvation only comes in half-gallons and union solidarity.

However, I garnered enough that I considered myself a believer. Not in a certain faith or sect of worship, I trusted that there's some higher power somewhere that made us. I never believed for a moment this higher power can or would influence the destination of our lives if we prayed enough or lived by their code. Danny roughly felt the same and we raised our children as non-church going believers in God.

It's easier to raise kids with religion, honestly. You can comfort them with a promise of heaven after they experience their first loss. You can say, "Well, God wanted it that way." when they ask an unanswerable question.

The concepts of Heaven - or worse, Hell - are the main reasons I would never call myself religious. Especially Christian after-life rules: we get eternal paradise if we believe a certain way and live a certain way and ask for forgiveness. How unfair to those who never get a chance to learn the rules. It's impractical and I wouldn't want to devote an ounce of faith to a God that would stack the deck in such a way. I guess I was more agnostic in my thoughts on the afterlife: I know enough to know I don't know.

But since that afternoon at Patty's grave, I'd been thinking about energy. I'm no scientist, but I know a couple hard and fast rules. First, everything and everyone is made of energy. Second, energy never dies. What if the thing we think of as a soul is actually just energy - the atoms and ions we have proven real and tangible - that creates our corporal bodies and then when we die, the energy transfers into the ether.

The energy of my dead son and my dead mom and everyone else we have lost could be swirling around us all the time and we'd never see or intellectually know the difference between it and regular old air.

On the same thought, energy follows a natural course. It flows in expected, formulaic ways. What if there are soul-mates, real life pairings meant-to-be, but it's more scientific than romantic. The energy in me had to find and pair with the energy in Danny or create the children we did and the lives we have. There's no predestination or All Powerful Being picking and choosing what is to happen to us, but instead a grand plan of the unknown universe where all matter follows its natural, beautiful, cruel course for eternity.

It's certainly easier to believe in than a God that lets a healthy 10-year-old boy die from a bee sting.

I realize Danny is staring at me in the mirror. I smile at him and point to my head - my code for 'oops forgive me, I'm heavily medicated' and trade him places for lotion time.

***

The smell hits me and I open my eyes to the brightness: it's snowing. I felt it in my bones before I fell asleep. I wake instantly and carefully sneak out of bed. I go to the window, it's coming down hard and fast - blanketing the earth in its pristine, waxen protection.

I love snow. It's the best part of living in Wenatchee. Sure, it can be a hassle and it's not like I ski or snowboard or even play in it anymore. It is just so insanely beautiful. I used to wake the boys for the first snow, every year. We'd bundle up and write our names in the fresh half inch or so and try to catch flakes on our tongues. I wish Patty were here to see this.

He is here, isn't he? He's in the air I breathe and the fat flakes falling on the lawn now. I quietly dress and debate on waking DJ. I would hate to worry him or Danny that I'm maniacal or spiraling. I loathe that I have to consider what others think of my mental state. It's depressing that I can't just be 'me', especially lately when I feel so good and free. I sneak out the front door, lift my chin and let the frozen missives from above fall on my face.

Invigorated, I turn around and quickly make my way to DJ's door. I tap gently as I open it. I make my way over to his bed and pull back the cover a little to shake his shoulder lightly. He stirs.

"What is it? Did I oversleep?" He mumbles trying to focus on his clock. DJ's gotten himself up since middle school.

"No." I smile at his handsome face. "It's snowing baby. Do you want to come out with me?"

His face contorts in confusion and exhaustion. "So?" He says forcefully. "It's 3AM, Mom." He pulls the cover back over his shoulder. "I'm not a little kid anymore."

I take a step back and whisper, "I'm sorry." I take a look around at the plaid and dark wood we'd decorated his room with a couple years ago when he's out-grown all the Star Wars paraphernalia. If it weren't for the back pack on the desk chair and the pile of textbooks, I would assume this was a grown man's room. No posters, no toys, no pile of dirty laundry. I take in the impersonal wall-hangings, save one photo. It's a small framed snapshot of DJ and Patty at the Apple Blossom State Fair, four, maybe five years ago.

I remember this. We'd all gone to the town's parade that morning and the carnival that night. We let the boys eat cotton candy and corn dogs and ride anything they wanted. We'd let them break away from us and ride with friends, they'd come back every hour or so for more money or tickets. Danny and I were fine to take the ferris wheel and sit back and people watch. I took this picture of them in front of the Zipper, the attraction Patty was most excited to ride. It was twilight and all the rides' flashing lights were starting to glow.

I remember being worried about the sobriety of the operator of the Zipper. I mentioned it to Daniel, how that man looks high or spaced out. Dan told me carnies aren't allowed to work sober and the boys would be fine. I watched that man like a hawk the whole time.

He had illegible knuckle tattoos. Not as in I couldn't read them, they could not be read at all. Almost as if they were crossed out messily. He was covered in grease and oil and his uniform shirt hadn't been washed, well, ever. It labeled his name as Clancy, but I had my doubts. His shoes were either brand new or well cared for, the white rubber soles were unblemished and perfect. Clancy appeared to be either 22 or 56. I absolutely could not tell.

How does one become a carnie? Did Clancy run away from home and become America's oldest trope? Was he a fourth-generation ride-operator? Did he join up through some temp agency, unsure what else to do with him and his tattoos?

Clancy has been a carnie for six years. He did join up in his home town after dropping out of high school. He decided to travel with them after he learned the joys of easy access to drugs and alcohol and the cute girls who work the game booths. Clancy's drug of choice is whippets and it's been wearing on him mentally and physically.

He wasn't always an after-school special. He was a bright, out-going kid and a decent student. His parents' divorce in 7th grade hit him hard. They both told him they loved him and it wasn't his fault, but he was sent to live with his awful grandmother while both parents 'figured out their next steps' and it sure felt like a punishment. Those next steps must have been awfully steep, as neither parent returned for poor Clancy. He was abandoned to his semi-senile, incontinent, mean grandmother's care until he signed up with Farris Traveling Carnival.

He has a new family now. Every night, after the work is done, they all sit around a giant fire pit and share drinks and smoke and sing ZZ Top and Whitesnake songs. Clancy is as happy as he can remember being and has a new tattoo - the whole length of his shoulders - CARNIE 4 LIFE.

I take one last look at the picture. I know why DJ framed and displays this one. It was a perfect day, one to hold on to forever.

***

Back in my room, after one last spin in the winter wonder out front, I silently undress and slip back into bed. I'm careful to not wake Danny with my freezing hands. I pull our thick comforter to my neck and think about the perfect day at the festival.

Patty was alive and I still day-dreamed. I wasn't delusional then. I really have done this my whole life, as far back as I can remember. I did it at six-years-old, the butcher at Ray's Market, I imagined he was secretly one of Johnny Carson's joke writers. I inspect the deepest cavities of my brain to understand why I would have assumed that.

It hits me: Dad laughing. My father has always been stoic but he laughed at the butcher's joke about sausage (something about a donkey's...oh - wow, just understood that one) the same way he'd laugh at The Tonight Show. I chuckle lightly at a child's perspective: only one man is capable of making my father laugh. My inexperienced mind made that connection and a whole backstory about the large man in a white apron. The story floods back to me. He wrote jokes at night at a wooden desk with one of those green accountant lamps and mailed them to California. Johnny only paid him a nickel a joke so he kept working as a butcher during the day. I remember imagining him having a beagle named Chuckle and a cat named Porkchop. It was brilliant, really. If I met a child with that kind of imagination, I would have praised it and encouraged writing courses or maybe theatre classes. I would make sure she had every opportunity to grow this gift.

I was never encouraged. I was just slapped on the back of the head and told to pay attention.

I think back to telling my father about my day dreams. He was half listening and said, "That's nice, kid." I tried to explain it to my mother once when she asked why I was always so quiet and inattentive. She looked confused and told me it was rude to make assumptions about people. After that, I kept my imagination to myself.

I basically kept everything to myself.

I think of the shopping bags hidden in the back of the pantry - I still keep everything to myself.

***

"You do seem good. You look good." Chrissy gave my new outfit a once over. I still feel a bit guilty about the clothing splurge but I was able to justify it to Danny - and myself - with how well everything fits. The meds kill my appetite. Evidently, being bat-shit crazy is an excellent diet. I didn't realize how poorly my old clothes were hanging until I tried on these new ones.

"Thanks!" I smile at her assessment and brush the smooth fabric on the thigh of my slacks. "I got some updated professional wear, as I may be looking for work soon." Danny'd finally told me that I wasn't getting my job back. The news stung briefly, but mostly I felt relief. I was miserable there.

"Do you feel ready to work?" Chrissy asked without registering her opinion. She's really good at that. I have noticed, by her lack of bias, how much I pick up on what other people want me to say. I didn't realize I was so accommodating, until forced to think for myself.

"I do and I don't. It turns out, according to my husband, I don't have to. We're 'financially healthy', can you believe that? His exact words: financially healthy! Weird, right?" I heave an exaggerated sigh with lightness in my heart. "But I can't see myself just sitting around. Especially since DJ's almost graduated. They don't need me around all the time. I've been thinking a lot about what would make me happy. Bri and I talked about it a lot this week. I have some ideas but haven't settled on exactly where I'm headed."

"I'm thrilled to hear you've reconnected with your friend." Chrissy said while jotting something down. "You need a whole support team, not just your family and partner. Do you feel supported by the friendship?"

"Absolutely." I answer without hesitation. "It's more balanced than it used to be. In fact, I think I talk more than she does now!" I laugh, but it makes me think. I do talk about myself a lot. I'm going to make sure Bri has a chance to vent or brag or just babble the next time I see her. Which is actually right after this session.

"Great, Nancy. Just great. I'm thrilled with all the work you're doing. This," Chrissy holds up and hands back my therapy notebook, 'is fantastic. You keep better records than any other patient I've ever worked with." I beam, a verbal gold star. "Let's make your goals for the next two weeks."

"Two weeks?" If I were a dog, my ears would have actually perked up. I look at her expectedly.

"Yes." She grins. "You've graduated to bi-monthly sessions. We're all on board; you're ready to take a step back. You'll still see Dr. Adkinson once a month too. He's got to keep up to date on your medications. You've made remarkable progress. Do you feel ready?"

I hesitate. And then I think about why I am hesitating. She looks at my furrowed brow with concern.
"What if I slip again? What if I don't realize I'm delusional or losing it and no one catches it until it's too late?" I didn't realize this was a concern of mine until the words leave my mouth.

Chrissy nods to acknowledge what I've said. She takes a beat and then says, "Honestly, there's a small possibility of that.

However, your support system is mightier than ever. And not just the addition of your rekindled friendship with Brigit, your husband now knows what to look out for and frankly," She considers her next words, "he has probably learned he was rather inattentive toward you before. I doubt he would let this happen again. Also, at any point, if you feel like you need more supervision or an extra session, all you have to do is ask."

Her words comfort me. I nod in agreement. "Okay. Thank you, Chrissy. I am ready to step back."

***

"Letting little Birdie flap her wings?" Bri teased. "You're uncaged! Free! Fly!"

I laugh. I'd just told her about my last therapy session. I was trying to have a serious conversation with her about how I need her to watch out for signs of my delusion returning or report to Daniel if she suspects I'm unwell. Of course, Bri makes it fun.

But not at my expense, Bri's humor always feels inclusive. She's the only person with whom I've been in on the inside joke.

"I did realize something, though, in my session. We always talk about me. Seriously. I have no idea what's going on with you. How are the kids? Brandon is graduating this year too, right? Are you still selling leggings?" I look at her, excited to hear what I'd missed.

The joy drained from her face. I'd never seen Bri look so serious. I am instantly anxious. Instinctively, I get closer and place my hands on her arm. She bursts into tears. I wait for her to let me in.

Bri proceeds to tell news I wouldn't have imagined in a million guesses. I wasn't the only one falling apart around here, but I hadn't given her a chance to tell me any of it.

Brigit caught her husband, Mike, having an affair. He wasn't sneaky or shy about it. Bri confronted him and he laughed in her face and told her he was leaving to be with this woman. He already had a lawyer and they're still in an ugly battle which Bri had already mostly lost. Mike got the house and 60% custody of the kids.

She tells me the only place she could afford was a dumpy downtown apartment and the kids hate visiting her there so she rarely sees them. They've sided with their dad, she thinks, since he was always the 'good guy' to her disciplinarian mothering. Bri unloads nearly two years of strife between sobs and gasps and moments of red-hot rage.

I look at her in awe. In these last few weeks, I've cried and moped and whined about every little inconvenience and my dear, sweet friend has lost everything. I hug her tightly and silently vow to help her, no matter what it takes, at any cost.

***

Later, after dinner and showers and my evening preparations, I make love to my husband in a way I can only call preventative. Not because I wanted to, nor because I felt like he wanted to, but a bodily plea for him to not stray from me.

***

Precision parked on a tricky one way; I prepare myself to exit my car for the third time. I look at my therapy notebook, consider opening it, but I know it doesn't have the answers. I am early enough to overthink here in my car for another five minutes if I want.

I'm just outside the front door of Impress Personnel, Wenatchee's top rated (only) temporary employment agency. Bri suggested it, she used them to get the medical transcriptionist job she has. She doesn't love it, but it pays enough to support her new modest life and she can make her own hours. I like the idea of trying on jobs before I commit. Or get committed.

I chuckle at my own joke. I'm spiraling a bit from nerves. This is my first interview in over 15 years. I look at my face in the rearview mirror: makeup is good, hair is fine. I know my outfit is appropriately business casual; I looked it up on the internet and basically copied the first picture. I have my freshly revised resume and my rehearsed answer for why I left my last job. I'm ready.

I'm also an anxious wreck.

I look left and right for something, anything, to save me from myself. A distraction, a sign from the universe, a brick flying at my head; I'm not picky. I see a man entirely too well dressed for this part of town. He's in a sharp black suit carrying a shiny leather briefcase. As he gets nearer, I can see it's not as nice as he'd like me to think it is. The fabric is thin, clinging to his body awkwardly and has the shine of a mostly poly-blend. His attractiveness pulls the look off though. He's a hundred-thousand-dollar man in a forty-buck suit.

He glances across the street briefly, and I see the profile of his sharp jawline. He opens the door to the temp agency and enters with the bravado you'd expect.

Of course, Jacob does everything with confidence. Always has, since he was young. The only son of Marlee and Greg Reinhold, Jacob was beloved and a little spoiled. Marlee dressed him in the finest clothes they could afford and made sure he attended Montessori preschool. Jacob observed how people were instantly nicer and more accommodating to him than some of peers. He deduced it was also why people would stop his mom and randomly compliment her on her adorable son. Jacob learned early that he was attractive and he didn't have to try all that hard to get by.

He was never outwardly rude or impolite to anyone. When his friends would mock the fat kid or make fun of someone with braces, Jacob would remain silent. He got a reputation for being a great guy, a humble Adonis. He was nominated and elected class president without any effort. In his tenure he did nothing but persuade his vice president into writing his speeches and doing all the work. He was equally lucky in his romantic life; girls would flirt and ask him out. He would show up and be polite and over time became Wenatchee's most sought-after young bachelor.

His mother made him apply to colleges and attend the closest state school, Central University where he partied and squeaked by on perceived charm for a couple years until his almost non-existent GPA forced the university to expel him.

He moved back home and bounced between his childhood bedroom and living with various girlfriends for the next few years. It always ended the same: the girls would realize Jacob wasn't what they thought he was. He wasn't a good listener: he simply didn't talk over you or interrupt. He wasn't a good lover, didn't have any discernible personality of his own, and he was objectively lazy. He'd never tried at anything and while looks and silence were enough when he was young, at 30 everyone around him found it unforgivable. His father had enough the 5th or 6th time the man had moved back home and served an eviction. Greg gave Jacob $200, a nice suitcase, and a dispassionate handshake while his mother sobbed in the kitchen.

Jacob sat on the curb for a few minutes and considered walking to his ex-girlfriend's house and begging for another chance. He looked deep into himself and knew he didn't want to do that, he didn't really love her, he loved how she took care of him. He knew his dad was right, it was time to grow up and do something, anything with his life. He checked into the cheapest motel in town and paid for a week, got a cheap suit at the discount department store, and made an appointment with the employment agency. Jacob Reinhold was ready to be held accountable for himself and be a real adult.

I'm inspired as I watch him through the glass door, being escorted into an office inside. How brave of Jacob to take these important first steps. If he can do it, so can I. One more check in the mirror and then I get out of my car and start my next chapter.

***

"Your resume is fine, your references check out, but I have one question," Shirley starts, "Why temp work? You could have found a reception job in an instant. I know for a fact there's at least 20 postings right now that you'd be perfect for. Some with good benefits and more security than anything I can offer." She looks at me curiously.

Shirley is exactly what I'd picture if you asked me to describe an employment resource agent. Khaki pants, nude flats, nice but basic button up, a string of modest pearls, and poorly dyed auburn hair in an over-styled helmet. I bet she has a cat that she loves a little too much. Oh, no, not now Birdie.

"I'm ready for a change, but I don't know what I want yet." I smile warmly at her. "I only had the one job my whole adult life. I want to know what's out there and an agency like yours seems like an excellent way to find out." She seems pleased with my answer.

"Most of our listings are labor jobs and agriculture." I take a deep breath; I know I'm not right for brick laying or picking fruit. I wouldn't survive an hour. "But, with your skill set and since you don't need full-time, I'll call you when we get office support and related listings. How does that sound?"

"That's perfect." I smile again. "I'm so excited."

***

I didn't need to wait long. Shirley calls me at 4:00 that afternoon. I'm needed at 9:00 the next morning. She gives me an address and tells me to dress comfortably but still appropriately. She has no other details except the job should last two days. I thank her and feel excitement wave through my whole body. I'm needed. I have a purpose. I will have an adventure. I will have something to talk about other than my meds and the cashier at the market. Elated, I text Bri the good news and get started on dinner. I can't wait to tell Danny.

***

Pulling in promptly at 8:45AM, I have no idea what I'll be doing today, but I have irrepressible optimism. It's one of our valley's huge fruit processing plants. I've driven by probably hundreds of times and I'm excited to see what's inside. It's all production and storage, what would they need an office administrator for?

There's a door to the side with OFFICE stenciled above it; I assume that's where I need to go. I open that door to chaos.

There's a man and two older women frantically pulling paper from boxes, handfuls of loose white sheets with erratic file folders here and there. The man looks panicked and the women are both annoyed and confused. Against my better judgment, I lightly clear my throat to get their attention. The women look at me, more annoyed than before. One says, "The retail store is on First Street, sweetie."

She pegged me right; I love that retail store. I buy an entirely too large box of fresh cherries there every summer. The boys and I eat them until we get sick.

We used to, anyway.

Undeterred, I say, "I'm here from Impress Personnel." No reaction.

I try again, louder. "I'm here from Impress Personnel." Nothing. They've already mentally dismissed me as a lost housewife. "I'm your temp." Still not getting them to care.

Again, louder: "I'm from the temp agency. You asked for help from Impress Personnel." I'm getting nowhere.

"I'm your damn temp!" I yell.

That gets the attention of all three. They look at me, suddenly relieved. The taller of the two women comes toward me like she's going in for a hug. She takes my arm, and pulls me into the paper hurricane. "Why didn't you say something? We're so glad you're here!"

She guides me to the man. He offers his hand. "Hi, I'm Ned Sones: like Jones with an 'S'." I shake his hand. He didn't have to tell me how to pronounce it. This is Sones and Sons Fruit. They've been in Wenatchee as long as anyone can remember. "Hi." I say, trying to look and sound confident, "I'm Nancy Caulkins. I was told you guys can use a hand." I look around.

"Yes, quite the mess, I know." He sits on the corner of the desk behind him. "You see, we're in a pickle. Do you have payroll experience?" He looks hopeful.

"I do. I've handled payroll for my last job for over a decade." I think back to the parking lot outside, there were over a hundred cars. "But that was a small office. You've got a great deal of employees, I imagine. What system do you use: ADP? QuickBooks? PayrollPro?" I'm mentally crossing every finger I have. QuickBooks is easy, even with these kinds of numbers.

"Sorry, sweetheart, I don't know what you're talking about." He lifts his hat and runs his hand on top of his hair. "Over my head! I grew up in this industry, I can grow 'em, harvest 'em, sort 'em, and ship 'em. I can fix any machine in this place. I love the fruit and I love this warehouse. But I was never one for paperwork or numbers. I left all that stuff to Irene."

I look around, "Is she sick?" I'm hoping she can at least email me some information.

He looks down. "My auntie Irene died two days ago." He pauses. "God rest her soul."

The two women murmur a quiet, respectful, "Amen."

"Oh, I'm so sorry." I don't know what else to say.

"Thank you. It was time, she was quite old. I'm glad she's with Uncle Pete." He straightens. "Anyway, sweet old lady kept the books here since my dad was in charge. And I thought we would be fine, as she had these two as her assistants and they could just take over." He shoots a callous look at them which they meet with equal contempt.

"She wouldn't let us do anything!" The taller one defends. "Old bat wouldn't even let us answer the phone." She looks ready for a fight and then looks suddenly at her feet. "May she rest."

"You could have warned me, Fern!" Ned tosses back. "You too, Cathy." I mentally note: Tall one - Fern, like the plant. Stouter one - Cathy, like the comic.

"Ok, ok." I say, trying to break the tension and understand what these people need from me. "I'm guessing payroll is due?"

Ned nods. "In two days. And we have no idea how to even get started."

I take a deep breath. I did want to try new things. I wanted to feel needed. This fits the bill.

"Let's get started." I say with a grin.

***

It takes me about an hour to get into a groove with Fern and Cathy. They were stepping all over me and each other, differing responsibility and tossing blame. The best system was for them to sit at their desks and do nothing except shrug or point when I asked a question. Irene's desk seems to be under this mountain of papers and files, but they're dusty. This isn't where she worked, it can't be.

"Where did Irene actually do her work?" I toss to the ladies. Fern points at the front counter, where I see a well-worn stool. I thank her and look over to also see what seems to be an old, leather ledger and an ancient calculator. I walk up and touch the buttons, so worn the numbers are no longer visible.

Irene was old school. I bet if I open this ledger, I will find pretty much everything I need. I nestle into her beloved stool and try to feel her energy. This is the one place of order in the whole office. I open a small drawer to my right and find some pens, nicer click-tops with black ink, a corporate checkbook, and a small journal. I reach for the latter, but her energy stops me. That journal isn't pertinent to the job at hand; it's private.

I look back to Fern, who I have determined to be the more competent of the two, and ask, "Where are the time cards?" She again points, and I follow her directional prompt to a tidy stack in a wooden box on the counter. I know of these systems, never used one, but I have a good idea how Irene managed all this. I pull the top time card off the stack. I see a name neatly written at the top, Gerardo Riviera - 19887. I assume it's an employee number. I'd ask Fern but I already know I will just see her shrug. Below is a table of the weekdays with times punched on two 'in' and 'out' columns. I'd never once in my life punched a clock but I'd seen it in so many movies, I can hear the sound.

Gerardo punches in at 5:59 every morning. He takes lunch at 10:30, give or take a minute or two, but is equally punctual about coming back at 11:00. His end of day varies from 4:00 to 5:15. Punctual Gerardo works hard and some quick mental math puts him at seven and half hours of overtime this week. I get a sinking feeling in my stomach when I think about federal withholding, social security, and other taxes. Did Irene calculate these for each employee, every week?

I prepare myself to open the ledger. It's massive and probably has all the tax and overtime rates as well as a running ledger for every single employee. There's a thick ribbon bookmark about halfway through the book and I decide that's as good as any place to start.

It's far less complicated than I'd feared. I opened to the records for last week. Tidy, meticulously written rows of employees by number, hours worked, and amount paid. I see no column for overtime, no taxes. The sinking feeling expands to my chest.

"Fern, do you get a W2?" I ask without turning around. She's silent. Eventually, Cathy squeaks out, "We're family. We're all family. Labor laws are different for family."

Deep breath. "Does any employee here get a W2?" I already know the answer. I need to find Ned.

***

An hour later, I've got Ned's credit card and am headed to an office supply store for a company computer and some bookkeeping software. Once I got him to believe how dangerously illegal the current system is, he basically begged me to help them modernize it. I'm completely over my head right now, but determined the universe wanted me to bring Sones and Sons Fruit to code for a reason.

I remind myself of this while I'm setting up the desktop and the operating system, of course, takes a lifetime to load. I remind myself while on hold with the printer dealer, trying to get a decent commercial printer/copier delivered by end of day. I remind myself several times while explaining, again, to Fern and Cathy how to get the employee I-9 information. I'd worried this system was set up due to immigration status of the employees, but it turns out it was just how Irene had always done it.

And no one, not a single person in the last five decades, had questioned it.

While I killed time waiting for the bookkeeping software to load, I decided now was as good a time as any to eat the lunch I packed and get a bit nosy with Irene's small journal. I open my lunch bag and take out my turkey and avocado sandwich and settle in, hoping to find some answers or at least a good story. I open it to see it's definitely Irene's tidy cursive, and the latest entry near the back dated Monday.

Her death must have been sudden. I'm sitting on her work stool on Thursday. The last entry is short and leaves much to the imagination:

"All time cards accounted for. Once again, I think Patrick McDaniels has someone punching in for him, will investigate. Remember to pick up ink for ink pads."

Ever watchful, that Irene. I imagine the woman setting up a sting. An elderly woman crouched in a cardboard box next to the time clock, waiting to catch the man in the act. I'd heard Cathy mention to Fern what a shame it was that Irene didn't hold on one more month, she'd have made it to 70-years-old. I wonder if she picked up the ink. I snoop a few more of the old, apothecary style drawers in the counter. I find various stamps, ink pads, and a nearly empty bottle of ink refill. I make a mental note to pick up some more; I feel like Irene would like that.

I feel oddly indebted to the woman. I'm changing almost everything she'd established and managed for fifty years. I owe her at least the satisfaction of one last task completed.

***

"DJ, I appreciate this so much." I say again.

"Mom, it's no big deal. I can boil some raviolis. I'm nearly an adult." He sounds exasperated with me and my gratitude. I take it down a notch.

"Right. Well, sad to miss raviolis and dinner with my boys. I've already told your dad I will be pretty late. You didn't have anything I needed to take you to tonight, right?" I'm suddenly fearful I'd missed something.

"No. But…" He teases, "You wouldn't have to worry about stuff like this if I had my own car."

I smile. His dad and I were just discussing this. I don't want to get his hopes up though. "Good point." I say. I see the printer delivery guy pull up. "I gotta go baby. I love you."

"You too." He hangs up. He was never a big fan of phone calls. At least he didn't ask me a thousand questions like his dad did. Daniel was rather concerned that my temporary placement two-day job turned into a possible all-nighter.

I understand his concern. I contemplate how I would feel if I were in his shoes as I let the delivery guy in. My wife goes off the deep end, has a make-believe son for over a year, gets help, gets better, and then calls you randomly to say she'll be working well into the late evening, possibly early morning. I can see where that would raise an eyebrow. However, I don't have time to worry about it, I've got work to do.

***

I'd asked Ned if he could spare some of his workers to help me and he rounded up a posse. I'd hinted at him finding me younger, more tech savvy folk would be best, those free to work late. He brought me Brianna, Yolanda, and Mike. Fern and Cathy had managed to get the I-9 docs from every worker on site, surprisingly, and now were taking the show on the road to track down those who worked off-site and had the day off.

The bookkeeping software was, as I'd hoped, idiot-friendly and did most of the work. I had Brianna read me off information from the I-9 and I'd create an employee profile. I'd have Yolanda find that employee's information in Irene's ledger as far as rate of pay and Mike would find that employee's current time card so I could generate a paycheck and stub for each. My goal was to have every single paycheck printed and checked this evening, ready to go. I could then spend tomorrow teaching Fern and Cathy how to do it for next week.

Ned picked my helpers wisely; they knew when it was okay to make a little small talk and when to stay quiet. They only did as I asked of them and stayed out of my way. Mike seems young, barely out of high school. He's a tall, gangly thing with acne scarring and brown hair cut close to his scalp. Yolanda's too pretty to be here. She could honestly make a fortune modeling for a skin care line or as one of those people that make a living posting pictures on Instagram. Brianna is a smiley, curvy young woman with auburn hair. She reminds me of my old friend Shari. Pretty but probably mostly overlooked for being heavy, Brianna compensates with kindness and light-heartedness. I'm happy with our little team.
Once we get into a rhythm and I fully understand the software, we're able to get an employee entered into the payroll system in under five minutes. I'm relieved, at this pace it won't take nearly as long as I'd feared.

I wonder what Irene would think of all this. I'd peeped a photo of her in the main hallway, blowing out candles on cake. She was thin and angular and appeared tidy and proper. Her collar was high-buttoned and her posture perfectly straight, even caught candidly. Ned had mentioned her husband preceded her to the grave; I guess she'd been happily married for a long time. Did she raise kids? Was she as precise and unbending with them as she was the payroll of Sones and Sons? Did she keep a ledger of their misdeeds and accomplishments?

The late hour has me thinking silly. Maybe I should send one of the kids out for coffee.

***

Three and half hours later, we entered the last few employees. Fern and Cathy had returned with the remaining needed pieces of paperwork, complaining loudly. I heard their words but felt they also enjoyed being needed and useful. They both expressed excitement when I told them I would teach the system the next day. At least, with their eyes.

I held the completed stack, almost too large to handle, with relief and pride. I did this. I took chaos and turned it into order in the span of a day. A long day, to be fair, but they would have been completely screwed if the universe had sent Jacob in the cheap suit. I imagine a dignified 'thank you' from Irene as I set the stack in the safe. I left Sones and Sons Fruit with my tired head held high.

Chapter 8:

Once Shirley heard Ned Sones' ringing endorsement for my work, she promised to keep me busy. I reminded her I was hoping for less than thirty hours a week and had blackout times for my appointments, but she still called every day this week. I was happy to be needed, but recalled Chrissy's warning about balance. I was still rigorously journaling and started a new page with four equal sections for family, work, friendships, and health. I debated on making five, separating my marriage from my family, but decided against it. My marriage is great. Danny and I are a team emotionally and physically. If anything needs work in my home, it's my relationship with DJ.

I start there, writing 'DJ car'. Danny and I had just gone over finances last night and we can easily spring for a decent used car for our son. I was surprised looking at our savings accounts. Danny had described it as 'financially healthy', but it was much more than I would have guessed. There was a sad moment in the discussion when he told me, technically reminded me, we'd gotten a settlement from the life insurance policy we'd had for Patty. I immediately protested, saying that money should have gone to charity or the team and he reassured me that we'd donated a good part already. I don't remember, it's fuzzy. I do remember Coach thanking me for the uniforms, but my confused, broken brain assumed he meant sewing on patches.

I remember setting up the policies. Since I worked in insurance - everyone in the family had decent coverage. It makes sense, it's very little money to insure healthy kids. What a gruesome investment that was.

I asked Danny if I can take DJ car shopping, just the two of us. I explained how I felt our connection needed some repair given, well, everything. He hesitated. I could see the mild machismo rear up in him, rarely heard from. I smirked internally; Danny and I have the exact same amount of mechanical aptitude: we take automobiles to professionals. He agreed, asking that I please check in with him before buying. We agreed on a budget and DJ and I made a plan to start looking after school today.

I also write 'look up crock pot recipes' and 'family movie night' in the first section. My new job is unpredictable and I need to have easy meals ready to throw in the slow-cooker and eaten whenever. Family movie night is a call-back to the before time, back when there were four of us. We'd all cuddle on the couch and watch kids' movies or sometimes epic blockbusters. Danny would pick classic sports films sometimes; every once in a while, I'd sneak in a cute romantic comedy. I loved those nights. I hope maybe they can bring back some of our shared bond.

I move to the next section: work, but my phone rings and brings reality into the friendship section. It's Bri and she's inviting me over. I tell her I've got a couple hours before my therapy appointment and would love to see her. I love her small downtown apartment. It's ancient, but has incredibly high ceilings and giant windows and access to a cool rooftop patio. The situation may be tragic, but at least she's living in style. She hasn't furnished it much yet, but when I temp'd at a thrift store a couple days ago, I was able to buy her a gorgeous, vintage, green velvet chair and chic little birdcage to brighten the living space. I've also got some throw pillows I'd purchased for my bed that Danny hated. I'd held on to them for a while now, not wanting to get rid of them. The mustard yellow and burnt orange embroidery will be lovely with the chair and brown leather couch she already has.

She greets me with a bear hug and a huge smile but I can tell something is off. Her eyes are puffy like she'd been crying and she was in gross, old sweatpants and a holey t-shirt.

"Honey, what's wrong?" I hold her tight and she lets go. Through her sobbing, I hear more about her awful husband's lawyer and how she can't afford her own anymore. I listen as best I can, but also start to formulate a plan. Don't I know a lawyer? A woman: she helped other women, a real bad…no, that was a daydream. Wait, back at the insurance agency, we covered a lawyer that I always got along with, Ken. He'd bring me coffee and sometimes a pastry and we'd talk about unusual coverage situations. We were both fascinated by strange liabilities. He's a real sweetheart. I read in the paper that he did a divorce that was making national headlines - a football pro who'd retired in Lake Chelan. I bet he would help my friend; I could offer office or bookkeeping work to help pay her bill.

Before I know it, my phone reminds me I have to go. I promise her I will text her tonight and check in tomorrow. It kills me to leave her like this, but I have to keep balance.

***

"Wait." Chrissy interjects, "You basically started a whole

payroll system from scratch in two days?!" She sounds incredulous, possibly skeptical.

I don't blame her. It sounds like fiction and I'm well, the most remarkable thing about me is that I'm a real good liar. "It's not as challenging as it sounds." I start reassuringly. "The software is simple. It was the same way I did payroll at my old job, just a few more people. I had a great team. These programs make it completely fool-proof." I start to worry about how ludicrous it would seem. She's right, I'm just a crazy mom with no education. I probably messed it all up.

"Nancy," She interrupts my thoughts. "You don't need to undersell yourself. You should be proud. I'm more interested in what you learned from the experience." I give her a quizzical eyebrow movement. "You decided to go with the temp agency to try on new jobs - what did you like about that one? What didn't you like? I think temping is an excellent idea for you. Let's recap, let's find your path from it."

She's exactly right. This journey: the jobs, the therapy, everything - is about discovering who I am and what makes me happy. "I liked leading my little team. I got lucky; they were all fantastic. Well, the kids were." I chuckle. Fern and Cathy were fine in the end but it was like pulling teeth at first. "I've never managed before. I think I'm good at it." Chrissy nods, encouraging me to go on. "I don't think I would want to work in the fruit industry. Almost everyone was making minimum wage, and none of them earned overtime before this week. I can't imagine how hard that work is - for a few bucks? It's depressing."

"And what about the other jobs?" She asks simply.

"Well, the thrift shop just needed someone to run the register while they reset all their displays. I didn't enjoy that. Boring, didn't pay well. It did remind me how much I like that aesthetic: vintage and kind of funky." I think back for a moment. "Wow, I almost forgot about the day I was at the cola dispensary. The warehouse was huge and loud and everything was sticky." I couldn't wait to shower after eight hours of working. "I was just shredding old documents. It was boring as well. I did notice that most of the employees seemed happy, like they were friends."

"Were you not friendly with your co-workers before?"

"No." I think about why. "I guess not. I didn't really have anyone on my level there. I was treated like a receptionist when I was really an office manager. I wasn't happy, especially at the end. Well, I wasn't really there though." It's the truth. I was in a delusional state. But also, I didn't have peers there, mostly men, no one close to my age. I'm happy I don't work there anymore.

She's looking through my journal now. She gets to my unfinished page about balance. She nods encouragingly.

"Nancy," She smiles and hands it back, "I'm pleased with your progress. I can't wait to see how much more you make in the next two weeks and beyond that. Please be proud of yourself."

***

Friendship and health getting little checkmarks for the day, it's time for family. Specifically, car shopping with DJ. Danny and I had looked at some advertisements and some car dealership websites last night and came up with a few cars that met our list of requirements. We wanted to get him something with good gas mileage but nothing too sporty as we didn't want him to get a taste for speeding. Nothing too big or tall, but, again not a tiny import as it's Wenatchee and winters can be brutal. Of course, we wouldn't be buying a newly licensed 16-year-old a brand-new car, but also nothing older than he is. Daniel had added nothing red or weird on the list too, but I didn't think that was a deal-breaker. If we find a perfect car at a perfect price and it happens to be red or lime green and my son loves it? We're getting it.

This is a belated birthday gift too. I'd missed DJ's birthday while I was a lithium-zombie. I was physically there, but I wasn't. I'd missed him taking and passing his driver's exam too. It was a few weeks, but I feel like I missed so much. Especially after everything else I'd missed while I was a wackadoodle.

DJ opens the passenger door and climbs in. His usual stoic demeanor is softened and I can tell he's excited. I am too. I ask him if he's hungry.

"No, not really. I ate lunch." DJ says as he puts on his seatbelt.

"In my centuries of experience," I say, chuckling, "One should never make any major decisions on an empty stomach. Let's swing through the drive-thru coffee place real quick. They have muffins, bagel sandwiches, donuts. We can grab you a snack and something to drink. I sure could use a coffee."

"I've never had coffee." My son says simply.

"They have way more than coffee. They have shakes and smoothies and hot cocoa, gah, the menu on the side is as big as they're little shack." I've been getting myself a coffee almost every day lately, sometimes two. I consider it self-care. DJ shrugs in a way that suggests 'why not' and we're off.

***

Two mochas, a muffin, and three dealerships later, I ask my son something I should have started with: "What do you want?" He'd been polite and accepting at everything we'd seen, would nod his head and say something nice, but there was nothing that seemed to cause a spark in him.

DJ shrugs and looks away.

"Honey, you can tell me. What kind of car do you want?" I put my hand on his shoulder.

"You'll say no. Dad already did." He's sullen, common for most teens but it's heartbreaking in mine.

"I promise I won't say no. I may not buy it for you, certainly not today, but I won't say no reactionarily." I plead.

"I really want a motorcycle." His face lights up.

Panic. Dread. Over my dead body. Not in a million years. Say something nice, you promised. "Oh, wow." I raise my eyebrows but try to keep my face neutral. "Like a little speed one or a big, loud thing?" I can't even begin to imagine which answer I would prefer right now. Breathe, Nancy. It's going to be okay.

My son is more enthusiastic than I'd seen him in ages. He pulls some magazines out of his backpack and starts showing me this model and that color and talking a mile a minute about engine size. I had absolutely no idea he liked motorcycles, let alone knew anything about them.

"You'd have to take a special class, right? And get a different kind of license?" I ask, trying to process.

"Yeah, there's a couple places that offer motorcycle safety. It's not all that much more expensive than my regular driver's ed was." We'd made DJ pay for driver's education on his own, so he knew exactly how much it costs. He'd made the money working at the Boy Scout camp last summer.

Deep breath. "Okay, I will talk to your dad. But son, I hate to get practical here, please look at this stuff on the ground? The dirty white mounds all over, remember those?" I'm teasing and pleading. On top of being incredibly dangerous, there's snow here one to three months of the year.

"Yeah, I know. I would get a cheap car or maybe a truck too. For when the weather is bad. A truck makes the most sense, so I can tow my motorcycle when I move."

When he moves. That hits me like a truck. I just processed losing his brother and now my DJ is already talking about moving away. In his truck with his motorcycle in the bed.

Another breath. "Ok, let's talk to dad."

"He'll just say no again." DJ looks defeated again.

"Yeah, I can see why too. But it's not solely his decision." I mean it too. I don't want this kid on a motorcycle ever but I also know what it's like to be 16 and feel like no one listens or cares. He's a great kid and deserves to be at least heard.

***

No checkmark on the work section today, there's no way I can balance all four every day. I decide I like this system for me, a check in to make sure I'm not devoting too much of myself to any one part of my life. I sit at my desk and go over my journal, checking that I recorded my meds and all pertinent information. I've just had a less than pleasant discussion with Daniel and he's already gone to bed - skipping lotion time to make it clear he's distraught. He can be itchy, for all I care. He was being closed-minded and not really hearing me.

I don't want DJ on a motorcycle. However, I can't stop him from doing so when he's 18, in two short years. I can spend those short years setting him up for safety and letting him know I value his interests. I will get Daniel on the same page. Eventually.

***

The line for coffee is four cars deep. Absolutely worth it; I'm celebrating a successful meeting with the lawyer I knew from the insurance agency, Ken Brennan. I was thrilled he remembered me and agreed to meet so quickly. He was enthusiastic about taking Bri's case and when I brought up working in exchange for payment, he just shushed me - saying he'd get the money from her cheating husband or wouldn't take a dime.

It was also good to see him again. I'd forgotten how much I enjoyed talking with him. He never treated me like a ditzy receptionist. A part of me was a little hopeful he'd take me up on my offer to work for him. But that's not what the universe wants for me right now. It wants me to patiently wait for this mocha and then report to duty at my next temp job: Valley View Custom Glass. Shirley told me it's a half day and that they're regulars with the agency. I'd not heard of them before, but I've never needed a new windshield or anything like that.

I arrive 15 minutes early, as intended. I have a spotless record with my new job and don't intend to harm it, even for a small job like this one. I'm curious what I'll be doing. Probably stocking or inventory, I assume. The building isn't what I expected. We're in the industrial part of town which has been gentrifying lately, new brew-pubs have been coming in, taking advantage of the old brick and concrete surfaces. It's a short building made of painted gray cinder blocks, with a giant mural wrapping around to the side. It's psychedelic nonsense, but pretty and colorful. The building sits behind a large warehouse, unseen by average Wenatchee citizens.

I open the heavy door, pushing past the literal gravity and my invisible circumspection. I see a showroom with giant glass-doored cabinets filled with vases. Oh, my dear lord, those are not vases. My breathing quickens. This is a drug den. Those are drug pipes. All sizes, colors. Some as tall as my waist. I don't know where to look. I shouldn't be here.

"Can I help you?" A man appears, he's bearded, shaggy, wearing a flannel shirt. He belongs here. I do not.

"I." I stop as soon as I start. I have no idea what to do. I guess it's legal now. I see new recreational marijuana shops popping up all over town. They have to be careful how they advertise so they have clever names like Destination 420 and Day Tripp Farms. The man is still looking at me.

"It's hot in here." I stumble over the words. I just realized I was burning up.

"Yeah," he says. "We've got the oven on and JoJo's blowing up a storm. Are you here for something you ordered or just looking around?"

Right, I have a reason to be here. I swallow hard. "I'm Nancy, Impress Temporary Services sent me." But they shouldn't have. I didn't realize I needed to specify that I'm a sober prude.

"Ahh, right on." Bearded man says. "We could really use a hand. How are you with a tape gun?"

"Gun?" I reply startled. And then I process what he means. Tape gun, as in packaging. "Oh, yeah, I can tape a box. Show me where you need me." And please get me away from these drug pipes. He leads me to the back where it gets hotter and weirder. There's loud, rhythmic dance music playing and a huge open fire oven against the back wall. There's a woman holding a long, metal rod into the flame.

She's immediately enchanting. She's wearing an orange jumpsuit with a wide red belt, thick black boots, and her hair is woven into tiny braids and the braids into a thick, tall bun on her head. She's dancing with the pole and the fire and impossible to look away from.

The Beard sees me staring and says, "That's JoJo. Are you familiar with her work?" I shake my head. I'd always wanted to try glass blowing. Daniel and I were going to take a class on our honeymoon, but never found the time.

"She's amazing." Beard says with admiration in his voice. "She's one of the most respected glass artists in the world. We're so lucky to work with her. I've been apprenticing for six months and I still pinch myself every day to make sure I'm not dreaming."

I realize I'm still staring and force myself to stop. I look at Beard expectantly. He's still staring at the artist. I should probably ask him his name at some point.

"Right." He says, breaking away from her trance. "We've got a system going over here." He walks me to a side room, filled with boxes and packaging materials. "We have way too many orders to process ourselves right now. JoJo had another video go viral." He rolls his eyes. "Damn potheads. Don't even appreciate the artistry. Just wanna smoke out of a set of fuckin' mermaid tits." He picks up a beautifully made mermaid, her tails swirled with deep teal and sky blue. "This is hand-crafted borosilicate glass made by an actual legend and some stoner is gonna use it for a couple months and break it." He sighs.

"No," Interjects a thin, moody girl who appeared from nowhere, "It won't break because it's borosilicate and made by an expert." She's smarmy and sleek, I instantly like her. She turns to me. "Are you the temp?" I nod. She turns to the Beard. "She doesn't care, Jeremy. No one cares. Stop fanboying and wrap the mermaid tits." She pushes the piece firmly into his chest.

"Hi, what's your name?" Back to me.

"Nancy." I offer my hand. She glowers an implied rejection.

"Nancy. I'm Stina. Jeremy will package. You will tape. I will label. You will then stack," She points to her left, "over there. Questions?"

"Stina, Stina, no need to be rude." A voice comes from the other room. JoJo has entered. She's wiping her face with a towel and walks to me. "Forgive her, Stina was raised by yuppies and never learned interpersonal skills." She smiles and offers me a hand. "I'm Jolene Cosgrove. But call me JoJo. Did I hear your name is Nancy?"

"Yes." I smile as I shake her hand.

She pulls me closer to her and puts her other hand on my elbow, almost an embrace. Her voice softens conspiratorially as she says: "I lived for Nancy Drew books growing up. I wanted to be her. I wanted to wear sweater sets and solve crime. God help me, I changed my name to Nancy one summer while visiting my grandmother in Florida!" She releases me and looks me up and down. "A real Nancy. Are you inquisitive? Intuitive? I bet you are. All Nancys are a little magic."

"Did the kids give you a tour?" She continues without a beat. She's leading me now back to the oven area, her arm on my back guiding me. It's the most intimate I've ever been with a stranger but I don't feel uncomfortable. JoJo instantly ingratiates herself to those around her. "Have you ever blown glass, Nancy?" She turns to me.

"I really wanted to try once. There was a class on the coast, but we didn't get around to it." I must sound so lame to this woman.

"Ah! That's how they get you!" She laughs, giving me the loveliest smile I've ever seen, perfectly outlined by her bright cherry pink lipstick. "It was the same for me! I saw a man on the Oregon coast, blowing glass for tourists and I begged my father to let me take a class. He told me no; glass work was for rich, white men. He hadn't learned yet that I took things like that as a challenge!" She laughs again, percussive bells of glee. Were she to bottle that laugh, pharmaceutical stocks would plummet.

"How did you end up in Wenatchee?" This is a question I always wonder about people and so rarely ask. I'm especially curious now, the area only has a tiny population of Black Americans. Not to say we aren't diverse, at the last census Wenatchee was 55% Latino.

"Oh, I wish that was a more romantic story!" She props herself up to sit on a counter and face me. "I would say I followed the love of my life here while he pursued his skiing career or I moved here to take care of an ailing extended family member. I do wish it were a better story. I grew up in Tacoma and when it was time to build my own studio, I was priced out of almost everything. I started looking in more rural areas and then a real estate agent suggested Wenatchee. The buildings were more affordable and the cut rate power…can't beat that. Of course," She gestures back to the oven, "that beast takes natural gas, but the kilns are electric and I save a lot of money there. Plus, it's like living in a fuckin' Hallmark movie!" She gestures around. "I mean, look at this place. It's a movie set."

She's absolutely right. Wenatchee is a gorgeous valley, nestled against the North Cascade Mountains with the flawless, powerful Columbia River running right through the middle of the town. Every view, in any direction looks like photoshop. I'm lucky to live here. I need to remind myself of that more often.

The Beard, I mean Jeremy, loudly and obviously clears his throat. He's right; I'm here to work and there's much to do. I head back to the boxing area.

"Nancy?" JoJo calls to me, "Why don't you come by some other time for that lesson you never got to take?"

I get to work under the bossy but experienced leadership of Stina, my mind whirling with possibility and awe. I watch Jeremy carefully package the masterpieces, each special and brilliant. I don't doubt for a moment JoJo's offer was genuine, but why would I waste her time like that. I'm nobody. I'm the prude that freaked out because she saw a bong.

Truthfully, I'm still a little nervous even holding them. I keep half-expecting the cops to bust in and tell us all to freeze.

Five hours later, we finish packaging all the pieces and load them neatly into the showroom for the UPS pick-up. Jeremy nods at me in thanks, off to worship at JoJo's feet, I'm sure. Stina wordlessly tells me I can go with raised eyebrows. My time with Valley View Custom Glass is over. At least for the moment.

***

I hope to catch JoJo in the parking lot, smoking a cigarette. Partially so I can bum one, I've been craving them all day, partially to get reassurance she made the offer in earnest. No such luck, the parking lot is empty save some fat squirrels suspiciously eyeing me from the corner. They've clearly got a food source nearby, something a bit heartier than seeds. They aren't scared away by me walking closer and take a protective stance. They only scurry when I'm a few feet away and not far, watching me. I see their stash behind the dumpster: a mountain of mini corn dogs.

"Where did you get these?" I ask them softly. They do not answer.

I look around and see the new brewery that everyone is raving about. They have a neat neon sign on the window informing the public they have Snow River Pear Cider. I love cider. I used to make the boys and I hot apple cider every autumn when our front yard tree started to turn yellow and orange. I had never had pear cider. I wonder if that brewery is the source of the squirrel's greasy hoard. I walk over to find out.

I'd been to a brewery before for a co-worker's birthday. It was slightly awkward at first, but I'm always a bit anxious in large groups. I worried that people would think it was weird that I wasn't drinking alcohol. No one even noticed. I am hungry, and though I'm sure Danny saved me some chicken and rice, that doesn't sound good. I'm with the squirrels; I want to get fat on mini corn dogs.

Good fortune greets me at the door: a 1950's style cigarette machine. Perfectly restored, the mint green metal gleaming. I don't think twice before finding my wallet. I'd always wanted to use one of these. The machine accepts my ten-dollar bills and I'm rewarded with a satisfying plop when I pull the lever. I chose the light 100s. That's what my mom smoked.

I survey the building for a moment, a huge brick-walled space. The exterior wall is mostly garage doors. I would bet they open those in warmer weather to outdoor seating. There are long tables made from old shuffleboard desks lined with tall, metal stools. The bar has classic built-in swivel stools and I consider sitting there for a moment, but that feels too drinking-at-a-bar for me. I see a small table in the corner that looks perfect. I sit and before I have a chance to get nervous, a man approaches me. I assume he's waitstaff by his short black apron. He confirms this by pulling out a notepad as he asks me how I'm doing tonight.

"Fine, thank you. First time here," I start. "You don't by chance have mini corn dogs, do you?"

"Yes! We do!" He smiles. "They're my favorite. You want some?" He's prepared to write. I nod enthusiastically. "Do you want anything to drink with that?"

"I saw the sign for pear cider out front. Is it good?" I ask.

"Oh-em-gee, so good!" He pulls the notepad to his chest. "My favorite is the lemon basil." That sounds weird. I suppose my face shows my doubt and he continues, "But the strawberry mint one is just as good. Want me to bring you a sample? See if you like it?"

"That's so nice! Yes, thank you." He smiles and writes some more. "Um," I start, suddenly nervous for no reason. "I was going to step outside for a moment, is that okay?"

"Oh, sweetie, of course. I'll make sure no one snags your table." He's such a nice man. I am definitely tipping well. I sneak outside to break open the plastic cellophane and take a few illicit drags. I feel too conspicuous out front, so I step over a little and duck into a small alcove. It's an entrance to something unmarked but I doubt I'll trouble anyone here.

I reach deep into the secret, zippered pocket of my purse. Usually home to tampons only, it has housed the lighter I bought a few months ago when I played hooky from work and felt so free. It feels somehow like just last week and years ago. A lot has happened between then and now. I look at the lighter for insight, three inches of baby blue plastic. It shares no wisdom with me tonight. One more drag and then I head back in.

The waiter meets me at the table with two tiny glasses, no more than two or three ounces each. "You have to try the lemon basil too. Trust me." He says as he sets them down. "The strawberry here on the right, it's got that slight pink to it? And the lemon basil is over here. Flag me down when you're ready to order or if you need anything. They should be throwing your food in the fryer soon." He's already walking away when I'm about to express surprise that they're cold. And carbonated, it appears, I think to myself as I pick one up. I take a sip.

This is not what I expected. I've only had hot apple cider - pear cider is tart and dry. I take another look; I grabbed the lemon one first. I take a second drink and it's sharp and this time I get the lemon and basil. It's weird and funky. Then I try the strawberry, slightly sweeter, but still sharp, tangy. The mint hits after I swallow. Cold cider, like sparkly juice. Wild. I take another sip of each and decide my sweetheart waiter is right, the lemon-basil is better. I get his attention and point at the lemon. He gives me a thumbs-up and turns back to get me a full glass.

***

I don't recognize the music playing into the void of the large space. There are banjos but it's not country and western. I think I like it. I remember hearing about an app that can tell you what song is playing and try to download it, but my attention is stolen by a text from my sister. I hadn't seen her since before I'd gone off the deep end. Danny must have scared her good, she hadn't bothered me for money or babysitting the whole time. All I get are variations of this text: 'Just checking in. Love you and hope you're doing ok'.

I reply, 'I'm great, kid. Better than I've been in a long time. Maybe we can visit soon?' I mean it too. I miss Candy, even if she is a needy trainwreck.

"R U home?' She sends. I chuckle to myself. She would never believe the truth. Sweetie waiter comes back by and asks if I'd like another cider. Why not, I say. It's a lot of sugar, sure, but also refreshing once you get used to it.

'No. I am getting some food. Just got off work' Oh, man, would she have a laugh if she knew where I worked today. Maybe I should call her. Maybe I should invite her here.

'Me too. We were slow and my boss sent me home early. This is weird, but are you in the industrial district?' Whoa. How did she know? Does Danny have a tracker on my van?

She answers before I can ask. 'I saw your van. Are you at New Brew?' Oh, Christmas, what do I say? Oh, who cares. She can see me drinking juice and eating children's food.

'Yeah! They have great mini corn dogs. Come join me!' I pause for a moment before I hit send. She might ask questions I'm not ready to answer. I don't have much cash on me. Then again, she handled Dad this whole time too. I owe her. Moments later my sister walks in, incredulous.

"How did you even know about this place?" She says, taking her coat off to sit down. She's still in work clothes, a tight, black, low-cut shirt and black pants.

"I'm not a cloistered nun, you know." I nod at Waiter when he holds up a glass, wordlessly asking if I'd like another. They're really so good. "I was working just around the corner, my new temp job, you know. It was late, this place was open."

She looks stunned by it all, her pretty, black-lined eyes wide. They narrow as she looks me up and down. "You look," She pauses, seeking the right word, "different. Not in a bad way.

You lost weight, but something else." She leaves the thought in the air with the banjo music and echoes.

"I feel a lot better. I was pretty messed up, Candy." I take a sip and slide the remaining few mini-corn dogs toward her. She waves her hand. "How much did Daniel tell you?"

"He said, Nance, are you sure you want to talk about this?" She looks around.

"I'm not ashamed. I needed help and I got it. My therapist, Chrissy, told me how people have poor eyesight and there's no shame in getting glasses or contacts, right? My brain needs help. I got medicine. I am getting therapy. It's working."

"I hadn't thought about it that way. You know, I had a pretty bad problem with anti-anxiety meds, a while back?" I shake my head. I knew she was 'on' something, but assumed it was something harder, street drugs. She continues, "My doctor gave me Xanax like they were vitamins. Got me all fucked up. Those things are addictive. Be careful, okay?"

"Did you get help for your anxiety?" I ask, not wanting to intrude but curious. I'd never told my sister my struggles, nor did I know she suffered as well.

"It was rough, dude." She takes one of the rejected dogs and pauses to take a bite. "I don't have much support, my girls' dad sucks, our dad super sucks, and the one person I could really lean on, well, you were, you had just," She trails off. She doesn't want to say it.

"I'd just lost my son?" I ask softly. She nods. I reach across the table and take her hand.

"I'm so sorry I wasn't there for you." I feel a tear welling in my eye. She looks like she's near tears too.

"No, don't be sorry!" She cries out. She composes herself. "You have nothing to be sorry for! I feel terrible that I was so wrapped up in my shit, I didn't catch on to what was going on. I've been a real shitty sister. I treated you like an atm and I was so selfish. Nancy, I'm so, so sorry."

The waiter comes with my cider and hesitates. He doesn't want to break up the moment, but also wants to make sure my sister is taken care of. I suggest she have one of these ciders. Her jaw drops. "Nancy, when did you start drinking?"

The waiter takes a step back but stays close, trying not to be obvious but not wanting to miss a moment.

"Oh, it's not beer. It's cider. Sparkly juice. It's weird but really tasty. Try it!" I offer her the glass.

She looks at me and then the waiter, whose lips are pressed closely together, and then back at me. "Nancy. It's hard cider. It's alcohol. How did you not know?!"

I look at the glass in horror. I'd tried a sip of alcohol once, by accident. My dad's whiskey. It burned my mouth. This didn't taste like that at all. "Are you sure?" I ask her, and then look at the waiter for confirmation. They both nod.

"If you'll excuse me, please. I need a cigarette." I don't wait for an answer. I head outside.

Right behind me, Candy hurriedly puts her jacket on. "You smoke?! You really didn't know it was alcohol? What is going on Nancy?! Do I need to call Daniel?"

That stops me dead. "Oh, God, Daniel. No, please don't. He wouldn't understand." I make sure she can see how serious I am. "Please, Candy, this has to stay between us." She nods, still stunned.

"What a day! First, I was basically a drug dealer and then I got drunk!" I take a drag. "What the..." I stop myself and then roll with it, "fuck. What the fuck?!"

Candy stares, unsure where to look, what to say, or how to process. She grabs my pack and lights one for herself.

"I don't think I've ever heard you swear before." She finally says.

"I guess I'm mouthy when I'm drunk." I say with self-pity.

"Nancy, calm your tits. You had like, two hard ciders. They're 5%. You're not drunk." She says, rolling her eyes.

"I had three." I say, unsure if the things I'm feeling are the alcohol or shame of finding out I've been drinking it. My cheeks are flushed and I feel warm, despite the freezing air. I had noticed before Candy got here that I felt loose, easy, less achy than I would normally feel after five hours of manual labor.

"Oh, three? My bad, let's get you to rehab!" She cackles. She's enjoying every minute of this.

"I can be roommates with Aunt Peggy." I say sarcastically and she doubles over. Peggy is sister to neither our mother or father, but somehow our 'aunt'. She's a drunk who finds herself in rehab annually and comes to make amends and encourage Dad to quit drinking. She usually stays on the wagon a couple months, falls off, gets into some sort of trouble and goes back to rehab. At this point, she's practically the Yelp of recovery centers, she'll tell you about the mattresses and food, which ones have the best staff. Good ol' Aunt Peggy.

My sister and I share a look and I realize I hadn't laughed like this with her since we were children. I can tell she's thinking the same thing. We wordlessly embrace and head back inside. I need another round of mini corn dogs, a glass of water, and some time to process the events of today.

Chapter 9:

"I can't believe you got me a good lawyer, for free. Birdie, going loco may have made you a little magic." Bri says, still in disbelief. "He's handsome too, did you notice?"

I scoff. I guess he's not bad-looking. I really don't look at men like that. "He's not totally free. You'll have to pay him if he wins."

"Yeah, yeah." Bri has already moved on. She's examining the glass orbs on the coffee table I'd brought over. Inspired by my time with JoJo, I'd dusted them off from their storage in the garage. I'd purchased them on the honeymoon from the glass blower on the coast. I was fascinated by the blue and gold swirls and didn't care about the price. I got various sizes in different hues of blue. I'd put them away ages ago when the boys were at that toddler-ruiner phase and never put them back on display. I'd found a gold wire basket to display them in and gave them to Bri. They suit the growing chic aesthetic of her downtown apartment much more than my muted, neutral home. Friendships section: check, a visit and a gift.

"How's things for you?" Bri asked, her eyes not leaving the compelling globes.

"Pretty good. I accidentally got buzzed on alcohol, bonded with my sister, packaged drug paraphernalia, and got Danny to agree to get DJ a truck." I said it all casually and smiled when Bri looked up in complete shock. I filled her in on everything in the twenty minutes we had before I had to report to today's job.

***

Checking the 'work' section of my plan for balance, I arrived at the downtown location. I'm in front of one of Wenatchee's oldest structures, the Gaines Building. Once a grand hotel in the 20s, one of our town's tallest buildings, but decades past its prime. It has now been converted into affordable senior living. Shirley, as usual, didn't have a great deal of detail for me, just that this was a private job, the job order from a person - not a company. I briefly panicked that this, given where I was, would be some sort of day nursing or elder care job. I'm not qualified for that.

Nor would I want to be. Lots of girls from my class in high

school went into nursing. Our community college offered a respected nursing degree. Many of them worked as nursing assistants in high school. I would hear stories about changing hygiene pads and adult underwear. No, thank you. I applaud those who can; I know I cannot.

I take a deep breath and remind myself that Impress and Shirley have not let me down and that I am on a journey and there might be things that make me uncomfortable along the way. I open the doors to a once-beautiful vestibule with deteriorating, ornate molding and faded floral wallpaper. There's two, old, brass elevators on the right and an office on the left. At the far end of the entry: a sofa and a loveseat currently occupied by two older women with walkers, chatting away. I wave modestly when they look my way and head toward the office.

Immediately, I'm greeted by a tall front counter and a familiar smell. It's a perfume my mom wore; I forget the name but it smells like roses and mothballs. It's rather dark for an open office and I don't see anyone. I ring the ancient bell on the counter. A chair toward the back turns and I hear a voice say, "I can't help you. There's a girl coming soon and she will." The chair didn't turn all the way, remaining in its position facing a couple monitors on a desk.

"I think I may be that...girl." It's weird for me to refer to myself as a girl, I haven't in decades. "I'm Nancy from Impress Personnel."

"Oh, thank God, you're finally here. I have been waiting forever." The voice beyond the chair exclaims. It's 4 minutes before 10:00AM, the time I was told to be here.

"I'm happy to help." I say, fake smiling. "What do you need me to do?" I look around trying to guess. I see some stacks of files, nothing extraordinarily messy or clearly in need of my clerical skills. I will not wipe anyone's bottom today, I swear.

"Come over here, let me see you." The voice says. The voice is feminine, but throaty and crusty. I am a bit spooked but acquiesce. Walking over, the perfume smell gets stronger and slaps me in the face with nostalgia. Mom wore this perfume almost every day. When she was at her sickest, barely over a 100lbs, she'd wear this perfume to cover the stench of dying. I would love to turn around, walk out, and never come back.

But the universe wants me here. I approach. It's a woman, older, short silver-haired and petite. She's wearing large, dark sunglasses and holding the side of her head. "I need you to be me today." She says. "I got this stupid eye surgery and can't do anything. So, I'm going to sit here in the dark and tell you what to do. Are you competent? I told the gal I needed one with a brain."

I'm unsure how to respond. The glasses and the grouchiness make sense with this information. "I'm pretty competent. Where can I get started?" I say softly, in case she also has a headache.

"Aren't you a little old to be a temp?" She asks. "Are you a boozer? Criminal?"

"No, ma'am." Normally I could say I never drink, but last night proved otherwise. I'm certainly not a boozer or criminal. "I just needed a change after 15 years at the same job. Wanted to see what's out there."

"OK, good. We have a lot of elderly residents and they're easily bilked. I won't allow that." I like that she's protective of her people. I get that. She does need to take it down a notch. Look at me: I'm walking Christopher and Banks ad, not someone to worry about. I wait for her to answer my question.

"Well, I guess you can't cause too much trouble in one day. When you're not actively helping someone, you need to watch these monitors. These are from cameras all over the building." She moves over for me to better see. "Really pay attention to these four bigger boxes, but all of them too. See," She points, "This is just outside the entrance, this one is just inside, and these two are the elevators. This is where most falls happen. And," She pauses, "Incidents."

"Incidents?" I look at her. "Like what?"

"Oh, not to gossip but these fogeys act like this building is a disco sex club. They make out and get frisky in the elevator, it's terrible."

"Oh." I pause to consider why that was and then get a terrible mental image I try to shake. "What do you do when you catch them? I mean, kissing isn't illegal."

"Getting frisky leads to falls! Keep up! And heart attacks. These horny codgers are bound and determined to die and not on my watch, honey!" She works herself up and grabs her head again. "The rest of the cameras are the hallways, there's two per floor. They fall there sometimes, but not nearly as often."

"Can they kiss in the hallways?" I am half joking, half serious.

"Don't be smart. Now when the phone rings, you pick it up and say 'Gaines Senior Apartments, no vacancy'. Trust me. You will answer that question about 50 times today and it's smarter to say it right off the bat. Half the time they don't hear you or argue anyway. The rest of the questions you can put them on hold, you know how to put someone on hold?" I look over and nod, it's a very simple phone, "Ok, put them on hold and ask me and I will tell you the answer. Got it?" I nod again. "There are a few other things that may come up here and there and basic tidying. We can't put cameras in the lobby bathroom so I usually check them every hour or so. They don't fall in there much, but they sure can make a mess."

She thinks for a moment. "Oh, and you gotta shoo away any of them homeless that come in here. They'll try to use the bathrooms or hang out on the lobby couches. Don't give them an inch, they'll take a mile." She pauses. "Do you need to write this down, hon?"

I must have been making a face. I don't see what harm there would be in allowing people to use the restroom. I know public bathrooms can be hard to find and this building is in the middle of downtown. I shake my head no. I'm not going to argue; this woman is unpleasant without any added disagreement. The phone rings before she can insult me further.

I pick it up: "Gaines Senior Apartments, no vacancy."

A man on the phone says, "Yes, do you have vacancy?"

"No sir," I reply. "There's currently no vacancy." Old bat was right about this part.

"Do you know when there will be a vacancy?" He asks.

I think to myself: soon, if I don't watch the cameras well enough today. "One moment please." I say and ask the same of the woman. She rolls her eyes. "Tell him to call back after the 5th. Rent's due the 5th and that's usually when I find…anyway, tell him that."

I tell him and wonder what she was saying when she stopped. When she finds what? Oh, gosh. When they don't pay rent because they've died. I want to leave so badly. I watch the monitors instead. The ladies are still out on the couch. No one is entering or exiting, no one on the elevator. I see a man walking slowly on one of the hallway cams. I suppose I'll see him in the elevator soon.

"Excuse me, ma'am?" I break the silence. She nods, clearly annoyed.

"I didn't catch your name."

"Oh, yeah. I'm Deedee. What was your name again?" She still hasn't fully looked in my direction. I could have swapped out with a body double at this point.

"Nancy."

"Right, right. My head is killing me. I'm gonna head up to my place for a bit. Just watch the monitors, call an ambulance if someone falls. Answer the phone, no vacancy. Take a message from anyone else. And call this number," She hands me a post-it, "If you don't know what to do, ok?"

All 4'10" of salt gets up and walks out the door without another word. I watch her leave and then see her head to the elevator. I take her seat and watch her from the monitors. It's oddly compelling, watching someone traverse whole building floors through the sections on the monitor. The man I saw earlier in his hallway went to the elevator, somehow managed to avoid falling or having sex, and went to another apartment a couple floors down. Deedee's got a nice commute to the second floor, and is opening her door within a couple minutes. There's a tiny chihuahua leading a man down the hallway on the 5th floor, eager to get outside. There's a man outside asking for change and the old ladies on the couch were in desperate need of some.

***

About an hour later, there's a man outside the entrance acting strangely. He's pointing at the sidewalk and talking enthusiastically. There's no audio, but he appears to be shouting. There's no one else around and he's growing angrier at the spot he's pointing. He's a large man. It's hard to tell on the screen but much larger than anyone else has been in that spot. He's got a shaved head and I think I can make out a couple small face tattoos. He doesn't appear interested in the building or coming in, but I keep an eye on him.

I can't help but wonder if he's in a mental health crisis. That could have easily been me a few months ago, talking to an imaginary son. This could be drugs, I suppose. Perhaps it's an emotional moment of grief. This is the corner where his beloved dog was killed by an inattentive driver. He's heartbroken and yelling at God and the driver and his dog for not listening and society itself. I know that anger. It fills your every cell until it bursts out of you, a rage balloon. I screamed at the leaky outdoor faucet as if it had, somehow, killed my son.

No one was around to witness my outburst on CCTV. Imagine if it had been: it'd be a viral video - Middle Aged Woman Loses Her Marbles.

"You gonna work or just stare at the TV?" Deedee's rough voice breaks into the room. I turn in the chair.

"How are you feeling?" I deflect.

"Awful. Don't get cataracts, if you can avoid it." She makes her way toward me and I hop out of the chair to offer it to her. She swishes her hand to decline and reaches on the shelf above the screens. I hadn't noticed it there. She reaches for a little box and pulls out a small bottle. There are some pictures in frames and other brick-a-brack. "Forgot my eye drops." She snarls. "I'm going back to my place. Just." She stops and thinks. "Just answer the phone, take messages, close the office at 5:00. Lock the door on your way out. Shouldn't need you tomorrow. So bye."

I watch her leave and then peek at the photographs. The most prominently displayed is a dog, a very pretty long haired white and tan something, obviously at a dog show. She's got a big blue-ribbon award on her chest. She's on a blue-covered table and looks proud. The same dog is with Deedee in the next picture, giving her kisses.

Deedee looks younger in the image, happier. Of course, I've only seen glimpses of the woman, and most of her face was covered in sunglasses. There's something familiar about her. Something, maybe the perfume, maybe her petite frame - she reminds me of my mother. My mother, however, would never allow a dog to lick her face. She claimed allergies, but I think she disliked the chaotic noise and mess of canine friends.

The next photo shows another dog, tanner on the ears, being walked on a leash by Deedee at what I assume is a dog show. Deedee had show-dogs, or at least showed them. Such a strange practice; I've never quite understood it. The phone rings, breaking me from my snooping. I pick it up: "Gaines Senior Apartments, no vacancy."

"Do you have any apartments available?"

***

"So, you just watched the security cameras all day?" Danny says with a squished face. I try to read if it's disbelief or disdain.

I quickly finish chewing my bite of pasta. "I mean, not just that. I answered the phone and helped people who came into the office." That's a fib; only one person came into the office and she was only asking if Deedee was okay. "It's important to watch the cameras, though. The seniors have a lot of falls." I omit the sexual element, for his sanity and DJ is also at the table half-listening.

"You don't have to work, Nance." Danny says for what must be the hundredth time. I know he worries, but it's starting to feel a little condescending.

"I want to, babe! I know today wasn't all that exciting, but this is how I'll figure out where I want to spend the rest of my working life." Chrissy and I talked about this: my next step. I need to figure out who I am outside of a wife and a mother, or I will feel lost when DJ is grown. I'm hesitant to say this around my boys, though. DJ doesn't need me to put my emotional needs on him and Danny would probably roll his eyes.

"Mom," DJ says, suddenly a part of the conversation. "Can I still borrow your van tonight? Does it have gas?" I smile slightly and tell him it could use some. It has plenty, but I love throwing him a little extra fun money when I can. He's just meeting his friends for video games - could probably walk - but he's a good kid and deserves to have fun. As I grab my wallet, Daniel suggests I take a gardening class. I take a deep breath because I can't imagine a world where I would enjoy that and am saved by my phone ringing.

It's Shirley, from Impress Personnel. I'm needed tomorrow at the Gaines Senior Apartments. She knows I am not available on Saturdays but Deedee insisted. Demanded, likely. I tell her I will be there at 9:00AM.

***

"I just don't understand why you couldn't say no." Danny says again. We've been passively arguing since dinner. I spit out my toothpaste and grab the rinsing glass.

"I chose to go. The lady is comfortable with me and needs the help. Did you have plans with me?" I say while pouring some water. Huffily, Danny pulls off some paper towels and wipes the mirror. I had spit tiny droplets, speaking before I rinsed. I quietly finish the task and thank him. I look at him expectantly. I want an answer.

"No, not specific plans. I was planning on getting a new router and you and I usually set up things for the household together." He raises his eyebrows in victory.

Yeah, together, right, I think sarcastically. We purchased the router we're replacing five years ago. He picked it out and purchased it on-line, I opened it and set it up with DJ's help. We used the factory password and Danny and Patrick vetoed it at dinner and we had a family vote. It ended up being a fun night. We landed on Patty-Cake's suggestion of 'nutmeg478'. Nutmeg is a tongue-in-cheek soccer term and the numbers were our address - backwards. Easy for us to remember; hard for others to guess. I hadn't considered the sentimental impact of the simple task.

I wrap my arms around him. "Can you pick up the new router and we'll set it up together when I get home? But I insist we set the same password." He softens.

"I just miss ya Nance." He mumbles in my ear. I melt into him.

***

The line at the coffee stand is much shorter on Saturdays, makes sense - less 9-to-5ers. These are casual coffee lovers, they're mostly here for the love of drink not bodily fuel. I'm both, I suppose. I'd save a great deal of money if I made it at home but I tried last week and Daniel complained about the smell and the machine taking up space on the kitchen counter. I thought it was attractive, the brass Italian contraption looked nice next to my unused high-end mixer. The machine lives at Bri's loft now with everything else I love but my husband dislikes.

I still haven't mentioned to Daniel my revived friendship. At this point, it's starting to feel like dishonesty. I fear he'd dislike how much money and time I'm spending on her. I fear he'd disapprove of a lot of the things that bring me happiness lately. And mostly, I fear that if I open up now, he'll see a mental illness relapse of some sort and send me back to the hospital.

It's my turn at the window. The employee looked annoyed to be there. I tried making small talk. She wore a delicate, gold necklace that said 'Derek' in a generic but pretty script and I was instantly excited. Girls with traditionally masculine names are so interesting to me. I ask her, thrilled, "Is your name Derek?"

"No." she returns. Nothing else, devoid of a hint of human personality. She finally offers a rebuttal: "My name is Anne."

"Oh." I'm a bit defeated, but I persist. "Your necklace says Derek."

"That's my boyfriend." She says in a tone that feels like a verbal eyeroll and she turns to make my order. I can't stop thinking about the necklace. It's a girl's necklace. Too dainty for most men or boys to wear. That means boring little Anne had that custom name necklace made for herself with someone else's name on it.

I have someone else's name, I guess. Daniel's last name, that is. Oh, so many years ago I agreed to love him for richer or poorer and became forever Mrs. Caulkins. It was only strange signing my new name for a few months and now it is as automatic as putting on a seatbelt when I get in a car.

I wonder how old Anne is; I wonder if she's happy. She could still be in high school already branded to her first boyfriend. She could follow my path and marry him next year, have two sons, and a lovely split level on the hill. Or maybe she won't. Maybe she'll ditch possessive Derek and go to school on the east coast to find a love of wake boarding and Latino men. She'll write for a travel site and see every continent before 30. People will call her Annie and always remember the bright, sunny ball of light they met briefly. Boring little Anne will find adventure and passion and never come back to Wenatchee or think of Derek again.

"Ma'am. Ma'am?" Anne interrupts her future. "Take your coffee." She hands me my drink and punch card with a one last, disgruntled grimace.

I prefer the weekday baristas.

***

Before I exit my van, I take a deep breath and release it slowly. I am mentally preparing for sass from Deedee and another day of staring at the screens. I did enjoy that part of this gig quite a bit. It was socially-acceptable people watching. I tried not to drift off into daydreams, as I couldn't risk missing a fall or some octogenarian tom-foolery. But I did briefly indulge my curiosity about the residents and their guests.

Today will be great. Deedee will be grouchy and hopefully leave and then I will get to watch people and then, after a quick check in with Bri, I will go home and spend time with

Daniel and DJ. I grab my purse, heavy with packed snacks and my mental health journal and head in.

The lobby's grandeur somehow diminished overnight. Today I only see the peeling wallpaper and carpet worn by decades of foot traffic. I walk into the open office door and see Deedee perched on the office chair like a flesh gargoyle, ready to pounce.

"You're on time today, what a miracle." She tosses at me. I'm actually nearly ten minutes early. I guess it's generational. My father has similar distortions of time.

"How are you feeling, Deedee?" I deflect.

"Like I did my eyeliner with a chainsaw." She coughs lightly. "I think I picked up a bit of a head cold as well. Damn hospitals are germ factories." She wipes her nose. "Same as yesterday, watch the camera, answer the phone 'no vacancy', try not to let the place burn down. Okay?" I agree to her terms and watch her exit on the cameras.

I pull out my journal. I've been less meticulous lately and have an appointment with Chrissy on Monday. I enter last night's and this morning's medications and stats. I also flip over to my life balance sheets and make the appropriate check marks and notes. Having recently reconnected with my sister has inspired me to check in with my father more often. I have a nagging feeling he's slipped so far at least partially due to my emotional absence. I know from the few Al-Anon meetings I attended that his choices are not my fault. The support group for family members of alcoholics has a motto "I am only responsible for my own actions", but I also could have been more supportive the last few years. I note the observation and decide to check in next week.

I check the monitors. No one is currently in the lobby; the halls are clear too. There are meandering pedestrians outside, downtown Saturdays are for leisure.

I text Bri and see if she's up for a quick visit later. She sends a funny gif back of bunny hopping excitedly. I'll take that as a yes. It inspires me and I send a cute 'I love you' gif to Danny. I see movement on the cameras. A woman on the fourth floor is exiting with her wiener dog, a lumbering, overweight little unit. It reminds me of yesterday's discovery of Deedee pictures above. I look at them again. She looks so happy and proud. I wonder why she doesn't have dogs now; this building clearly allows for pets. Perhaps she only showed them or judged them. I suppose you can love dog shows but not the effort and cost of owning one.

I never wanted to deal with the constant cleaning of pets. It's hard enough to keep my house clean with my sons. Well, son.

And it's much easier than when they were little. DJ is tidy and does his own laundry. That was a funny transition, actually. He started doing it himself, without prompting, at 14-years-old. I was flummoxed as to why he'd suddenly decided to take on the task but Danny had pointed out that boys have certain things they'd like to keep private once they reach that age. I was so sheltered, only myself and my sister growing up, I had no idea. I also started quietly stocking hand lotion and tissues in his room.

The lady and her fat wiener have made their way through the lobby and exit. He immediately, hilariously, lifts his thick leg and pees on the planter by the door. It clearly takes him a great deal of effort. I hope that thing gets hosed down regularly; I've seen countless dogs lift a leg to it in my short time here.

The phone rings. I answer, "Gaines Senior Apartments, no vacancy."

The caller asks: "Do you have any apartments available?"

***

A few hours later my phone dings and I see Daniel has replied with a winky face. Neither of us are big on emojis or texting culture in general. It's an efficient tool for communication that people use too much. I'm sure my missive caught him off-guard. I'm hoping to assuage some of the tension from last night. I'm hoping that he too sees the value in my pursuits of new challenges and experiences, or will some day. I'm hoping that in 40 years - when all we truly have in our lives is each other - we will be married by choice and not habit.

I don't want to be one of these single senior ladies at the Gaines Apartments, shuffling some tiny, aggressive dog up and down the elevators for potty breaks and watching game shows alone. Like the woman sitting on the lobby couch now - she's just waiting for passersby to talk to. She could be a widow; she could be divorced. She could be thrice divorced, forever lucky in love but hoping to land Hubby Number Four in the bacchanalia of this palace of affordable housing.

She looks like a Betty or Gloria to me. I bet she's a firecracker, too. She keeps her friends in stitches, always has. Her bright yellow, polyester jacket has buttons on the front I wish I could read. They're likely sassy sayings about being old. She's wearing compression socks and orthopedic, velcro'd shoes with her less-than-modest skirt. She's clearly on the hunt. Betty is going to find a man today. Or at least make a friend.

She's always made friends easily. She's out-going and funny. She was a flight attendant when she was young and married a pilot when she was 20. William Gerald Fields was handsome and strong and proposed over the Atlantic Ocean and they eloped in Ireland, consummating the marriage in a strange Bed and Breakfast above a pub. Betty and the handsome fly-guy tried their best but both their schedules were hectic and the lack of quality time together tore the union apart after a couple years. Betty left her first marriage with his wings pin, an expensive luggage set, and her returned maiden name.

Husband Number Two and her new career fell into her lap, almost literally. On a particularly turbulent early morning flight into Dallas, a first-class passenger attempted a quick run to the restroom, despite the seatbelt warning light. He crashed into her, hard, and couldn't stop apologizing. He offered to buy her breakfast and since she didn't have another flight until the next day, she accepted. His name was Roger MacLeon and he was a tall silver fox. They talked and talked, an instant spark. After a few clandestine dates when she was in town, the man offered Betty a job with his large oil securities firm. She hesitated, but her back was suffering from the rough airways. She accepted on two conditions: first, she'd be more than just a secretary and secondly, their dating status be private. She didn't want anyone at her new job to think she'd only gotten the position because of her relationship. She'd seen too many flight attendants fall into that trap, accused of sleeping their way up. He agreed and Betty moved to Dallas and moved into her position with the transportation department with ease. She knew more about transportation than the department manager, having been almost everywhere in her short 23 years.

She loved her job and dating Roger in secret was entertaining. They'd share meals in neighboring towns, just in case. One weekend he took her on a helicopter ride over the Grand Canyon and proposed. She accepted and they were married that spring on his extensive property. The troubles started almost as soon as the honeymoon ended. Roger wanted to start their family immediately, as he had a few decades on Betty. She wanted to work and travel and hadn't considered getting pregnant for a few more years. Roger and Betty argued constantly over the issue and she started drinking to cope. A few months later, he would coldly serve her divorce and severance papers the same day, locking her out of their shared home and evoking her access to the building where she worked. She could have fought for scraps but he had money, lawyers, and determination she lacked.

Betty licked her wounds back home in Sullivan's Island, South Carolina. The tiny beach town was healing and relaxing. The gateway into Charleston Harbor, the tiny town had lots of visitors coming and going. Betty got a waitressing job at a high-end seafood place in the evenings and spent her days walking the shore looking for answers and avoiding the harsh criticism of her mother. Betty's mom, Mary Margaret Turanto, cried when her only daughter wed outside of the Church the first time. She cried when Betty committed the mortal sin of divorce. She sobbed when she had a second wedding in Texas without family or God and was completely devastated to learn the second marriage didn't last. She spent her days praying for Betty's soul on the Rosary and questioning her daughter's choices.

One day on the shore Betty caught the eye of a fishing boat captain. He appreciated her long legs and was so curious about the lonely brunette, he came ashore specifically to talk to her. Betty was too heartbroken and suspicious of men to give him the time of day. The captain, Robert Hinds, liked a challenge and found out as much about Betty as possible to place himself in her eye-line as often as he could. He became a regular at the restaurant. He knew her neighbor and started visiting more often. He even learned where she got her hair cut and made sure he had an appointment in the next chair when she got a trim.

Betty was unimpressed with Robert's persistence. She's been pursued before and aggressive men would eventually become possessive or lose interest as soon as they got what they wanted. Overall, she was over the idea of romantic love. Betty could never know that Robert was different from the men she'd known before. She didn't know the profit losses he was suffering from spending more time ashore than gathering fish and shellfish. She didn't know that Robert's father died when he was 14-year-old and he started supporting his whole family before he could legally drive. She didn't know he'd provided for his mother and siblings ever since and made sure each went to and graduated college without debt. She didn't know his heart was as big as the ocean and his capacity for kindness was as endless.

She would first soften toward Robert one day when she came back from her walk on the beach to see him pulling her mother's weeds under her watchful and persistent supervision. Her mother looked pleased and at one point actually smiled, an action Betty had rarely seen. She walked by the scene, pointed out a dandelion the man had missed, and got ready for work. A few days later, she came home to the man cleaning out her mother's gutters. She asked him if he'd like a glass of water. It was an unusually hot day for the coast and he looked miserable. He accepted and climbed down to follow her into the kitchen.

The simple gesture wasn't lost on Robert, but he continued playing the long game. He would end up repairing the weathered fence and repainting the house before Betty finally asked him, impatiently, "Aren't you going to ask me out already?"

He smirked and replied, "Well, if you insist."

His kindness didn't stop once he got the date. They would date for a year before he asked for his mother's ring and her mother's blessing. She was hesitant but something told her this was her real chance at forever love. Her mother pulled some strings and although she couldn't have a real Catholic wedding, being a divorcee and all, they allowed her to wed unofficially at the church. Her mother finally approved and even gifted the couple the title to the plot of land behind her own. They honeymooned on Robert's boat in the Florida Keys.

Once home, they built a modest house and started building a life. The construction came together quickly. Robert had plans for his dream house at the ready, spending so much time at sea with only his thoughts and dreams. The second story of the home had a large balcony with a view of the bay, often called a widow's walk. Betty refused to call it that, horrified at the dangers of Robert's job. Betty okayed his every indulgence on the design as she only cared about the outdoor spaces and was thrilled to plant a small vegetable garden. Betty got a job in air traffic control at the small airfield in the next township. Robert had hoped she would join him in fishing, but they learned she suffered relentless sea-sickness on the honeymoon. She took quickly to her new job. Betty was smart and cool under pressure, perfect for this trade. She also joined the Ladies' Auxiliary League at the church, at her mother's insistence. She befriended other young wives and enjoyed the social events and community fundraising. That fall she used the yield from her garden and her experiences in Texas to make and can endless jars of knock-you-out salsa for the annual bake sale. The exciting, new entry was popular and she won an award for selling the most wares.

Robert and Betty had three years of married bliss when the idea of starting a family was discussed and approved happily by both parties. They decided to start trying after that winter's shrimp season, Robert's most profitable and time-consuming crop. He'd be gone most of December and January and when he returned, Betty would be fully off her birth control and ready for their next step. She told her mother of their plan and Mary Margaret started knitting immediately. They would need endless blankets and hats and booties, she knew. One stormy morning in January, toward the end of the season, Betty drove to work with a bad feeling. She knew when she started clearing Coast Guard medi-copters for emergency take-off that something horrible had happened. She asked one pilot if he could tell her the name of the boat and the answer confirmed her worst fear. She helped them navigate away safely and took off her headset and called her boss over. Tears in her eyes, she told him she had to leave.

She steadfastly drove home and prematurely used the Widow's Walk for the final and most ever appropriate time. Her viewpoint allowed her to see the county sheriff's cruiser when he turned down the street. She already knew what he had to say. Her whole future was over, as she knew it.

Her mother oversaw the sale of the home and Betty took a job in air traffic control Bend, Oregon. She chose it because it wasn't Texas, it wasn't coastal, it wasn't any place with a single memory for her. She drove cross-country in Robert's old truck, wearing his coat, and had no plan other than: run far and run fast. Bend Municipal Airport was tiny, only serving central Oregon and private planes. She rented a run-down basement apartment from a large Pakistani family, the Jamalis, who lived upstairs and gave her little peace or privacy but fed her delicious food she couldn't pronounce. She wanted to save as much money as possible while she figured out her next steps. She struggled with wanting to drink away her pain, but she'd learned from her time in Texas that wasn't the cure. She befriended co-workers and some of the aunties from her landlord's family and started feeling a little better.

Eventually, Betty decided Bend was home now. She started going to therapy and grew comfortable with being single. She joined a card group and played pinochle and hearts twice a week. She purchased a small home by the airport and invested her money in bonds. She had the proceeds from the sale of her home and a decent insurance payout from Robert's death and loss of boat. She calculated she could comfortably retire, on her own, at 60 or so if she kept working and saving.

She stayed close to her former landlords and considered them family.

One of those Jamali aunties would introduce Betty to her boss at the local credit union, Miles. He was a widower and equally unenthusiastic about dating again. Miles Fornsworth was a sleek, compact man with glasses and dark hair. He looked like he couldn't harm a fly. He also enjoyed card games and was a fine companion when she craved company. They'd hit the casinos in Western Oregon and sometimes Washington together, never spending too much, of course. They planned a trip to a large casino near Seattle when he proposed they share a room. She thought he meant for fiscal responsibility, but packed her good panties - just in case. Mild Miles proved a formidable lover, surprisingly.

Nearly a year into their arrangement, Miles proposed cohabitation. Betty was hesitant, of course, but she enjoyed his company and thought how economically fruitful sharing expenses could be for her. He stayed over often, was tidy and respectful, the situation made sense. She made him sign a lease and he wasn't the least bit offended. A decade into the relationship, she actually brought up marriage. Now approaching 40, Betty wanted the security of legal entanglement. She'd married for passion, for romance, and for love before. It was time to get real and she had found her partner. Miles agreed easily and they started a spreadsheet for budgeting the wedding, their shared kink. The aunties catered the frugal but fun affair. Betty wore a sexy blue dress and Miles wore his favorite navy suit. Her co-workers drank heavily. Mary Margaret cried from 2000 miles away, unable or perhaps unwilling to attend. Betty, now armed with middle-aged confidence, tried not to think about it being her fourth marriage but her final marriage.

The pair honeymooned in Vegas for the cards and excitement. The majority of their budget went to this trip and they ate great food and did very well at the tables. The bank manager and air traffic controller are perhaps the only people to ever leave Las Vegas with a modest profit. They came home and settled into the same routine they'd shared for the prior ten years, only now legally bound. Betty had her impressive gardens and weekly card games; Miles had golf in good weather and bowling in colder months. They took frequent trips and merged their investment portfolios. Miles would give her monthly dividend reports and she was pleased with his fiscal talents.

They shared the next seven years in mutual contentment. They rarely found reason to argue and it was usually something silly, such as forgetting to take the garbage to the curb. Betty was promoted to management and they celebrated with sparkling cider and getting a hot tub. She often thought of Robert and what could have been, the children her mother had already made christening gowns for, but pushed those thoughts aside. Clearly, that wasn't meant to be her life. On the eve of their eighth anniversary, Miles told her he had an early tee time at the country club, but would come back with breakfast sandwiches and they'd hit their favorite nearby casino to celebrate. She slept in and put extra effort into looking nice for their special day. She grew concerned when he wasn't back by 9:00AM. Miles was punctual to fault and she panicked after an hour without word. She called the club, they said he didn't have tee-time scheduled for that day. She tried to reassure herself that she'd misheard him or he confused the course, but as she called all the other establishments in town it confirmed what she already knew. He didn't golf that morning.

She called his work and the teller that answered sounded weird and stressed when she told Betty that her husband wasn't there. She got answers shortly thereafter when several police cars came down her street. No Widow's Walk this time, however. No remorseful officer, hat in hand.

Miles wasn't the man she thought she knew at all. He was under investigation for embezzlement from the credit union, and many other investors who trusted him. Betty was taken downtown and questioned for hours before she even thought to ask if she needed a lawyer. She called the patriarch of the Jamili family, as he knew everyone in town and would know exactly who could help. Her new lawyer was there in twenty minutes and got her out of the station quickly. The lawyer, Ken Dwyer, was sharp as tack and suggested Betty check to see if she was one of the victims of his fraud, likely wanting to know if he was getting paid for his work.

In a day full of stressful surprises, Betty was shocked to see her account balances. He'd left her less than a thousand in checking and wiped their savings completely. She looked down at the pretty dress she'd worn for their planned outing and felt like a complete fool. She asked Ken if he would take her to the Jamalis', as she couldn't bear the thought of going home.

In the coming weeks, Betty would learn the lengths of Miles' fraud and lies. He'd stolen nearly two million from the credit union he managed and twice as much from investors who'd seen the same forged profit reports he'd shown his wife. He'd taken out multiple lines of credit in her name and when they'd refinanced a couple years ago, she didn't know he'd taken a huge amount of interest out of her home and put it into separate accounts. Miles hadn't paid the mortgage in months. She was facing foreclosure on the home she'd once almost owned fully on her own and her credit was destroyed. The FBI was now involved, as they'd traced him traveling to the Cayman Islands, likely planning an early retirement in the tax and extradition haven.

Betty became a pariah in the small community. People were sure she had to know something and gossiped about their constant trips to casinos. She tried to blow off some steam at one of her card nights and the group's chatter eerily stopped when she walked in. No one would look at her; she wordlessly understood - she wasn't welcome. Even her beloved Jamalis seemed to keep their distance. Her mother had passed the year before and once again, Betty was completely alone. Ken's last act as her lawyer was to file for a divorce in absentia and free the poor woman from him, legally.

She packed a few mementos from her decades on Earth. A set of pilot wings, the beautiful diamond brooch from her time in Texas, her medal from the Ladies' Auxiliary bake sale and Robert's jacket, her mother's pearls, the gorgeous watch Miles had given her when they were married, a few days' worth of clothes, her makeup and personal care items. She was leaving her home for the bank to take, with everything inside. She knew she could likely sell some of her things, but she didn't have the energy to try. No job, no plan, she drove away.

She briefly considered ending her life but found herself appalled by the thought. She'd already committed basically all the other mortal sins, but that one wasn't an option. She looked at her gas tank, recently filled. She decided to drive until she ran out of gas. While driving she cried one last time for the sad, eventful life she'd lived. She was born Mary

Elizabeth Turanto but always preferred Betty. She was an eager Betty Fields, an excited Betty MacLeon, a beloved, hopeful Betty Hinds, and until the 90 days are over, a victimized Betty Fornsworth. She decided when she landed where the fates and gas mileage allowed, she would be just Betty. And she would choose happiness and hope, regardless. That tank made it all the way to Wenatchee, Washington, where she worked to rebuild her credit, esteem, and life. She was employed as a ticket agent at the small airport until her bad back forced her to go on disability. Just Betty moved into the Gaines Senior Apartments, started a card night, and continues to hold out hope for a happy ending.

The phone broke me from the compelling story of Just Betty. "Gaines Senior Apartments, no vacancy."

***

Deedee came to check on me around noon. I foolishly hoped she was relieving me for a lunch break but no such luck. She looked around the office, checking every drawer and surface for evidence of my maleficence or incompetence. She looked disappointed when she couldn't find anything to complain about.

"I'm so bored." She sighed. "Nothing good on the TV. I guess I might as well work. You can leave." She gestured toward the door.

"Are you sure?" I ask. "You were in a lot of pain earlier. What if-"

"I'll figure it out." She cuts me off. She's done with me.

I slowly get up and look around for what I need to gather. I don't understand my reluctance to leave. I feel somewhat defeated, perhaps because it feels like I've been fired. It feels unfinished. I want to know the whole story of this place and its inhabitants. I start with Deedee.

"Is this you?" I point at her pictures. "Did you show dogs?"

"Yes." She says shortly. "King Charles Cavaliers and Springer Spaniels. I had Best in Show twice." She softens slightly.

"I've always loved dogs." I lie. "How did you get into it?"

Deedee takes my seat. "My parents were professional breeders. I trained and showed dozens of show dogs. That was a long time ago." She trails off.

"Was that here, in Washington?"

"Who are you, a reporter?" She snaps. "Get out of here already."

Something clicks in my brain and I realize why she seemed so familiar. It wasn't her perfume. She's wearing the same button-up shirt I'd seen her in before. At the grocery store, months ago, before I found out I'd lost my mind. I'd imagined her a light-hearted widow and former court stenographer, living in Wenatchee with an old friend. I was so wrong in my assumptions about her.

"Do you need a map?" She asks curtly. "Out the door and take a right." I have been standing here in my revelation too long. I nod and make my way out, still stunned. I look over to the couches in the lobby, Just Betty long-gone and replaced by an ancient man with a walker. I feel anxious and lost. I leave Gaines Senior Apartments on the verge of tears I can't explain.

I get to my minivan and try to process everything I was feeling. I've been through every possible emotion the last few months, from profound grief and remorse to guilt and depression to hope and even pride and accomplishment. This feels different from it all. I suppose a part of me thought, assumed, my daydreams were somehow clairvoyant. Maybe I knew something about people that others didn't, perhaps I possessed a unique people-reading skill no one else did. I was special. My problem was a gift.

It's not. I'm a person that makes up lies to entertain myself. How deeply pathetic.

***

I pull into my garage readying my next set of lies to my husband. I can't tell him that I cried in my van downtown for a solid hour because I realized I was actually insane and not gifted. I can't tell him I went to the glass-blower, JoJo, for an impromptu lesson. I can't tell him how I needed her healing energy so badly I showed up and begged for heat and silence or how she understood and put me to work without questions. I can't tell him I went to Bri's after and laughed and smoked cigarettes on her roof terrace. I can't tell him I was free to do all this because I was fired from a job that was never really mine.

I can't tell him that I don't know if I love him. That I don't know if I ever did, that I was a child that was so lonely and broken that I clung to the first man who showed me kindness and affection. I can't tell him that it's pathetic that we've only been to two states, Washington and Oregon, in our whole lives.

I can't tell him that I hate our beautiful home, 2,300 square feet of painful memories and sometimes I consider burning it to the ground to force us to move. I can't tell him that I like smoking because it feels as physically strangling and painful as I emotionally feel all the time and the equality is comforting.

I can't tell him any of this. He'll hospitalize me forever. I prepare my cover story and walk into our split-level prison to make dinner and set up a router and pretend everything is okay.

Chapter 10:

Chrissy's concerned face revives my anxiety. I've been on edge since the events of last Saturday. I'd decided my deceit with Daniel was enough and I would be as honest as possible with my mental health counselor.

She gathers her thoughts, as she always speaks with earnest clarity. The pauses still concern me though I've grown more used to them. "Nancy," She starts, "Having a good imagination is not a symptom of your mental illness. Can I be frank, here?" I nod.

"You're a little sheltered. You didn't get to go away to college or travel. You left your family home to get married and start a family, correct?" I nod again. "That is a path some are very comfortable with. But it's a path that can be cloistering and repressive. Especially for someone who has intellectual or artistic gifts, which you clearly have both. I believe your day-dreams are fantastic fiction and if you could, I don't know, write it down in some way you could focus it into a career in fiction writing or screenplays or something. I'm not concerned you felt it was some sort of extrasensory gift. I fear you were never taught that story-telling is our oldest and most important craft as a civilization." She searches my face for understanding. "Nancy, it is a gift. Just not in the way you assumed. And it's okay to learn new things about yourself."

I nod again, unsure what to say. I got stuck on her calling me sheltered. She's right and I think I am ready to explore more of what this world has to offer.

"So, to be clear," I start, "This isn't relapse? No med changes?" I am nervous as we're about to remove the anti-psychotic completely from my regime.

"No, Nancy. Not relapse. Just growing pains. Keep journaling, keep learning, and go a little easier on yourself. Oh, and continue taking glass blowing lessons, if you can. I have a feeling that would be an excellent outlet for you." She hands me some papers and my journal. "Here's some of my notes for you to go over, since you seem a little overwhelmed right now. Breathe. You're doing great."

***

Bri is anxious, flitting around her loft. She's just met with her lawyer and they have a hearing next week. It seems the family court system will do everything to keep all parties from going to trial and they're likely going to settle everything in mediation. She's going to have to sit across from her ex-husband and his lawyer and try to work out money and custody issues. I think back to my thoughts in my garage. I might be apprehensive about certain parts of my marriage but I would hate to have to deal with all this.

Bri will be fine, though. She's much stronger and braver than me. We've been spending time setting up her second bedroom for the kids. It's actually the larger room, they should be able to share without problem. We've been adding other cozy touches to make the industrial, modern space feel more like a family home. The loft is huge and has these amazing, huge windows that let in so much light. She's lucky to have found this space, so affordably. It's quiet too, surprisingly. You can hear the traffic noises when the windows are open and occasionally muffled sounds from the cafe downstairs but not often. The adjacent loft space is shared studio space and fully sound-proofed. It's great people watching, the artists and musicians come at all hours to practice their craft.

The loft might be my favorite place in the world.

It feels ugly to be slightly envious of my friend right now. She's going through hell, a mother's worst nightmare.

Oh, wait. I had that. She's living a mother's second worst nightmare. The penultimate maternal horror.

***

After school, DJ and I decide to go check out a pick-up truck at a dealership. He'd picked it out, and although very plain and simple, it seemed to be in fine shape. As my son had predicted, his father wasn't hearing a word about buying a motorcycle. DJ and I discussed getting a truck now and then he could work and save to buy whatever he wanted when he was an adult. I liked the idea of him driving a truck - a safe, reliable vehicle that he could also help friends move and pick up furniture with. It would be incredibly helpful on the handful of harsh winter days Wenatchee sees every few years when snow dumps on us in feet instead of inches and the whole town basically shuts down. It's only every few years, but it's awful and only those with trucks or large SUVs are able to navigate until the plows make their way into neighborhoods.

The last blizzard that bad was when DJ was in second grade, of course. Patty was pouting because his kindergarten class was canceled but DJ and I got him excited to go play in the snow. We could barely open the front door, three feet of snow burying us inside. Daniel was out shoveling the driveway, trying to make it into work. It would be futile; the plows didn't hit our street until the next day. DJ and I shoveled for the neighbor to our right, an older couple. We wanted to make sure they had everything they needed and were rewarded with hot cocoa with peppermint candies melted into it. Daniel was grouchy about missing work until I lured him outside under the guise of a leaky gutter and our sons pelted him with snowballs. The four of us had an epic battle and then warmed up in the house under all the blankets we had. I didn't have much fresh food in the house and we made a silly, comforting dinner of mac'n'cheese and scalloped potatoes. We made no-bake cookies with Chinese noodles and ate them in a blanket fort where the boys slept that night.

It's so strange to me how I can remember that day almost ten years ago with perfect clarity but forgot my son's death for over a year. I remember talking Daniel into letting the boys sleep in the fort and promising I'd deal with the mess in the morning. I remember how that night, after we made love, Danny apologized to me for his poor attitude while he held me. I was still shaking, gasping for breath and glowing in the musk of our bodies and he was clear as glass, even, and direct. He pulled my chin up to look me in the eyes and promised to treat me better. I kissed him and told him treats me wonderfully. I was touched by his earnestness, but also slightly confused.

I remember staying up after he dozed off, thinking about how often he'd apologized to me or had reason to. I was perplexed by it. His grumpiness wasn't that big of a deal, and understandable. Daniel Caulkins prides himself on his work ethic. He never cancels on his patients; he prioritizes their health above everything else. I remember pulling the blue, flannel sheet up to my chin and repressing tears I didn't understand. I remember the confused relief of that apology. I remember the next morning I put on makeup and curled my hair and made my boys pancakes and felt light as air.

I can remember the red blouse I wore and Danny sneakily appreciating my rear end in my jeans and how he cheered when he heard the rumble of the plow and I almost cried. I remember his quick kiss on the cheek goodbye and tearing down the blanket fort. I remember every single detail of that storm but I have no recollection of how or when I picked up my son's ashes. I'd give anything to understand my broken brain sometimes.

"Mom? Mom." DJ apparently had been trying to get my attention and waved a hand in my face. I smiled apologetically.

"I'm sorry love. Was thinking," I drift off. "About you in a truck. You're almost a grown man now and I love it." I grin. "How was the test drive?" I'd been left behind, as the truck only seats two and the salesman had to go, of course.

"Great!" DJ answers with the biggest grin. "Your turn!" I couldn't possibly justify to Danny the purchase if I hadn't also taken it out for a spin. I take the key from the salesman and take a deep breath. I turn to say something to DJ about snacks in my minivan but see he's being treated to a table of refreshments by an attractive young lady already. I know they're eager for a sale, but the woman laughs heartily at something he said and touches his arm. I raise an eyebrow and remind myself that it's okay. He's not going to run off with her and elope because she gave him a bottle of water and flirted a little.

"I've never driven a truck before." I confess to the salesman, Marcos. He's a strikingly handsome man. We'd come to the dealership that hires straight from modeling agencies; I suppose. He's a fit, young Latino man with perfectly manicured five-o-clock shadow and gelled hair. His lavender dress shirt matches the pattern in his tie and he has a fantastic smile.

"There's a first time for everything." He says casually as he opens the door for me. He's smooth but I don't get the pushy feel from him I've felt at some of the other dealerships. Not yet, anyway. I'd read that cash buyers, like us, aren't as attractive to most dealerships, as they make the real money on interest. I had felt less pressure since I started mentioning that up front. He helped me climb into the driver's seat and showed me how to adjust it to my height and preferences. He pointed out how the utility vehicle lacked many of the modern, electric conveniences such as power seats or windows. It had been a fleet truck and well-maintained, but ordered as basic as possible. I was about to express that I don't think my son cares about those things when he expresses the advantage, fewer small motors and things to repair. I nod, this is something my father would point out.

The truck may be basic, but the seat is comfortable and the interior immaculately clean. I wait for Marcos to buckle and start the engine.

***

"Mom, I swear, I will take such good care of this truck. I can't believe this is happening!" DJ is grinning and almost jumping out of his skin with excitement. We've signed the papers and called the insurance agency with all the info. I wrote the check and everything was cleared with their cashier. We're waiting on the temporary registration and then my son can leave in his very first truck. I dig through my purse for something I've had since he started driver's education. It's a keychain, a simple silver bar with a personal engraving: *Please drive carefully because I love you - Mom.* He reads it with austerity and hugs me tightly.

"Mom, I promise you, so carefully. I love you so much!" I rarely see this kind of emotion from the boy. I understand. I was the same with my first car. It's a symbol of freedom, of adulthood. It's huge. "Everything is going to be so good, mom. It's really happening, isn't it?" He looks past me, to all that is possible and all that is to come. I wrap him in one more big hug as they pull the truck around to us.

I watch my son drive away, swelling with pride and hope. I gave him some cash and told him to enjoy himself, carefully, and to be home by 9:00PM. I'd have to mitigate some possible irritation from Danny and wanted my son to miss any fall-out and have nothing but the happiest memories from this big day.

***

I take a left when I should have turned right and I didn't process my choices until I was at my father's home. I had planned on visiting this week, but something drew me here, today, right now. I haven't been to this house unannounced or uninvited since I lived here. I pause at the door. I knock, despite my anxiety. I hear Dad coughing and yell "Just a minute!"

I wonder who he thinks this is. Does he have many visitors? I hear him mumble something vulgar and ready myself. I usually open the unlocked door and yell 'knock-knock', but I'm also usually expected. He opens the door angrily, wearing a dirty white undershirt and pants he'd clearly grabbed from the floor, buckled but the belt unfastened. He softens slightly when his eyes focus on me.

"Nancy!" He cries. His surprise gives way to indignation. "It isn't the fifth. What did I do to deserve a visit from her highness on this day?" He bows sarcastically. I open the screen door and ask if I can come in. He nods and walks back to his chair.

"Hi Dad. I hope I'm not inconveniencing you. I should have called." He grunts and eases into his chair.

"You still nuts?" He asks. "Do I need to call that rat bastard husband of yours?"

I start to answer. He interrupts: "You losing your mind was the damndest thing. I had told Candy, I had told that piece of shit Daniel, no one listened to the old drunk! I knew you weren't okay. They just assumed the ol' drunk was an idiot. Ha! We showed them, didn't we kid?" His face shows regret in his words. We did show them, Dad. My wrists still itch sometimes and I feel the cloth restraints of the mental hospital. We showed them, alright. I shake them now, compulsively.

"How," I start. I want to know how he knew. Did I talk about Patty to him, knowing no one would believe him. I'm not ready for that level of honesty yet. "How have you been, Dad?" I'm a coward, but I have no idea what I'm doing.

"Same shit, different day. I'm okay." He shrugs. "How are you, though? All doped up still? Candy's been doing my bills and stuff - I'm surprised she hasn't fucked it all up or made off with all my money. Can you look over my checkbook before you go?" I nod, subtly. Candy is much stronger than I've ever given her credit for and doing really well lately, but I should check - just in case.

"I don't remember," I start again. I want to tell him about the gaps in my memory but I also don't want to confide too much with him. "I don't remember what happened when mom died. I know you don't like to talk about it, but I only remember bits and pieces. How long was she sick?" I look at him pointedly. I do remember this, clearly. I am curious what he remembers.

"Your mother was sick much longer than you kids knew. Being female-troubles, she kept it from me for a long time. By the time she told me, she had a foot in the grave. She still took care of us for another half year or so. She took to her bed in the spring and was gone before it got hot out. You were a good daughter to her, as always. Dutiful Nancy, would make sure her mama was clean and as comfortable as possible.

You'd run me out of the room when she needed to use the commode, as if a husband had never seen his wife take piss before. I am grateful you were there, though." He pauses and takes a long drink. "She passed on a Tuesday. We knew it was close, but she insisted I not miss work. You were home from school; I think it was already out for summer. You called dispatch and they pulled me off my route. The funeral home was already here." He takes another drink. "You were how old? 17?"

"Sixteen." My voice is unintentionally coarse.

"Yeah, I guess old enough to handle it all. Candy was still a baby. I was tore up real bad. You know." He nods toward me. I do know. The man crawled into a bottle and never came up for air since. "I sold her wedding rings to pay for her headstone, did you know that?"

I shook my head. I assumed mom had life insurance for such things. I wondered where they went. I have looked for them, from time to time.

"My biggest regret was having to bury her without them. I had them wrap a piece of paper around her finger with an I.O.U." He coughs out a half chuckle. "We were up to our necks in medical debt with your mother's cancer and it and your sister's surgeries had wiped our savings." I'd forgotten about Candy's surgeries. She'd suffered terrible, near-constant ear infections and had a tonsillectomy and tubes put in her ears the winter before Mom died. "The funeral home wanted cash, right then and her life insurance was going to take months. I had to sell our rings and the silver we'd gotten for our wedding. I was humiliated. What kind of a man can't afford to bury his wife." He shakes his head.

"You took care of it, Dad." I say simply. "You did what you had to do to take care of all of us."

"Yeah, I guess so." He sighs. "Why do you ask? Crazy-pills give you fuckin' amnesia?"

I think for a moment. I reach over to his tray and snag a cigarette and his lighter. I move the sofa's ottoman closer to him and sit on it, lighting up and taking a big drag.

"Not amnesia. Just trying to fill in gaps." I say. He looks surprised, but takes a cigarette for himself and also lights it. I continue: "How did you know I was batshit crazy?"
***

The man hesitates at the door to the studio next to Bri's. He's got a freshly shaved head and goatee, the go-to for balding middle-aged men everywhere. It makes them look tough and most start collecting sunglasses and tattoos to complete the persona. An agent at my old job even started riding a Harley to compensate for it all. I thought it was ridiculous and hoped the other bikers all called him a poser behind his back.

I suppose we all try on new personalities in times of transition. Isn't that what I'm doing, essentially? Trying on new jobs and experiences and seeing what fits: I'm the mentally ill version of male-pattern baldness.

The man can't see me watching him from the window on the roof terrace. He doesn't know I exist. He's got a guitar in a case that looks brand new and seems unsure of everything. I deduce he's there for a lesson. His new hairline compels him to try to be a musician. I think this is a much better idea than buying an overpriced motorcycle or taking on a mistress. I also name him Charles but he's going to tell everyone to start calling him Dutch.

Dutch, née Charles Andrew Logan, moved to the area as a child from Miles City, Montana. His parents, Frank and Laurie, had saved and planned and were opening their dream diner on Hwy 97. His mom's pies drew in business from their first day open and his dad was one helluva short order cook. They'd dreamt of this location specifically since they honeymooned in the area and fell in love with the Wenatchee National Forest. The turn-key diner came with an A-Frame cabin on the property and the small family started establishing roots in the lush, rural community of Liberty, Washington.

Dutch went to school in nearby Leavenworth, a Bavarian tourist town. He played football and was second string for the unremarkable team. His grades were mediocre but he was still thought of as a good student. It was a low bar. He and his friends cleverly called the town Worth-Leavin' and he was set on moving to San Diego to work at SeaWorld. Dutch's grades and athletic accomplishments weren't enough for any of the marine biology programs he applied to and he decided a new dream was in order. He started the training program for wildland fire-fighting but the heavy equipment and exhausting drills were too challenging and he washed out after a few weeks.

He licked his wounds in the wooded cabin, reluctant to reach out to any of his friends after bragging about his future as a hero.

Wildland fires are a big deal around here; Dutch wanted to help. He'd calculated this secondary dream after seasons of serving the fire-fighters at the diner. He'd always admired them and was excited to join them. After a few weeks of letting him pout in his room, his father threw an apron at him and told him to get his ass in the diner's kitchen. The place was slammed, it was the start of ski season and folks traversing the major mountain pass loved to stop at the beloved diner on their way coming or going from the slopes. Dutch busied himself with food prep and washing dishes, as he'd done since he was little.

After a few weeks of working open to close, he started learning how to man the grill under his father's demanding and watchful eye. His mother feared the boy would grow too comfortable and asked him to go with her into town one day after the lunch rush. She handed him a large wad of cash, a packed suitcase, and a bus ticket to San Diego. She laughed and told him to stop living his father's dream and go follow his own. The wise woman told him he didn't need a degree to work at the SeaWorld gift shop or ticket booth. She kissed his forehead and sent him off with a ham sandwich and a piece of pie. Dutch Apple, his favorite.

The man would arrive in San Diego and walk straight to the hiring office of the amusement park. He was in luck; the human resources manager was from the Pacific Northwest and so charmed by his story she hired him as a trainer-trainee off the street. The very next day Dutch learned how to present cold, dead fish to Orcas in a way that was safe for both him and the whale and he felt the whole-body rush of being near the majestic animals. He worked at the park as a presenter and trainer for nearly ten years. Unfortunately, it's a job for young bodies and he retired at 27-years-old. He returned to the mountain pass diner, this time by choice. He would reconnect with a recently divorced high school flame and marry the next year. The divorcee loved Dutch madly and held his hand as he lost both parents and his hair.

He didn't want to cheat or join a biker gang, but when listlessness crept in he knew he needed something. He needed to feel the full body rush of scoring a touchdown or feeding a 20-foot whale. Watching his wife lose her mind over a guitarist playing a downtown festival inspired him to pick up a new skill.

If he ever opens the door to his tutor's studio.

"Pretty lil Birdie!" Bri calls out through her window. "Are you ready or what?"

I guess it's time. I am ready. I'm surprised she's in such good spirits for the coming meeting. I put out my cigarette and climb down into her loft.

"Oh, I'm ready. Are you?" I inspected her outfit. We'd carefully picked out a modest blue blazer, I heard somewhere blue makes you seem honest and you should always wear it to court. This wasn't court, but it was close enough. She turns and walks to the full-size mirror we'd placed on the long interior wall to reflect the windows. She looks perfect; under the blazer a perfectly pressed white blouse with navy polka dots and skinny navy slacks. She pulls me next to her to share the reflection. She squeezes my hand.

"Birdie, I need you to really focus. It's time." She is as serious as a heart attack.

I check my phone. We have plenty of time, we could leave in a half hour and still be early. I am driving her there and would wait just outside the conference room. I may not be able to hold her hand, but she will have my unwavering support. She pulls me to face her. "Sweet Birdie. This has been so lovely." She brushes my hair off my shoulder. "But I need you to listen and really hear me, okay?"

I shoot her a doubtful look. I am not the one who needs to focus today. I assume she's projecting, look deeply into her eyes and await further instruction.

"Are you ready?" She asks again, with emphasis.

"Yes!" I laugh. I had already told her I just wanted a quick smoke before we left. I straighten myself and keep her serious gaze.

"Birdie, you need to keep it together, alright?" She's holding both my wrists now, firmly. They start to itch. I nod. I will stay strong for her. "You have to keep it together, no matter what." She continues. I nod again, fighting the urge to laugh. Bri's right to take this seriously, but she's being a little dramatic.

"Nancy." Whoa, real name. She isn't playing.

"I will keep it together. I promise." I say with every ounce of sincerity I can muster.

She continues her hold on me, and nods in acceptance. She exhales slowly. "Birdy, do you know what day it is?" Oh, wow. Flighty Bri is worried I would choose today to lose it again?

"It's Thursday, the 21st." I answer simply. It has been a long, eventful week, but I know what day it is. I'd had a long, hard visit with Dad and later Candy. I'd spent a lot of time with DJ, both of us avoiding Danny's protest over the purchase of the pickup. I'd eased completely off one of my medicines and was journaling a lot and taking time off from temp jobs to make sure I adjusted without added stress.

"Where did you sleep last night?" I start to laugh but for once that wasn't a ridiculous question. I'd stayed here, at Bri's loft. She was nervous and didn't want to be alone.

"Nancy, who is going to mediation today?" I break free from

her grip, starting to feel anxious. I don't understand why she's asking me these questions.

"Sweetheart, we do not have time for this. You need to pay attention." I spin my head up. For some reason Bri sounded just like my mom when she said that. She's standing in the same place, a pretty, blonde statue. "Who has mediation for divorce settlement today?"

I take a shaky breath and release it. She holds my eyes hostage for an answer.

"I do." I say quietly.

"Great. Okay, and what day is it?" She repeats.

"Thursday, the 21st." I take another shaky breath. I want a cigarette. I take one out of my pocket and she blocks my access to the roof.

"In a minute." She says. "I need to make sure you're ready."

"I'm ready! Fuck, I am ready. I don't need judgment from you of all people." I shove past her and she follows me out.

"Birdie, you're going to have a rough time today. I need to make sure you can handle it. He is going to attack your mental health." Her hair glows in the sun. She's wiser than I ever thought.

"I was pretending it was your divorce to deal with everything." I confess.

She pats my hand. "Atta-girl. That's right. What else have you been doing?"

I breathe deeply. "I don't know. Working. Healing. Preparing."

"Don't get defensive now. We have to get ready." She says calmly.

I am not calm. I feel defensive. She's right though. Daniel's attorney has already filed motions to prove me incapable of making my own legal decisions. That was thrown out on Tuesday.

"I am sane. I have certified affidavits from three mental health professionals. My counselor, my physiatrist, and the third-party evaluation on Wednesday. Your lawyer," I stop, correcting, "My lawyer says they can't even bring it up."

"Right. But, sweet Birdie, there's more." She's still standing ramrod straight, unmoving. I'm so used to seeing her in a whirl of activity - it's unnerving. It's like when I found that dead hummingbird on my porch. Patty was devastated. He insisted we bury the poor thing and have a proper funeral.

"Birdie, I need you to say it."

I glare at her. "You're not real." The words feel gross in my mouth, like the dead hummingbird's lengthy tongue grotesquely limp and swollen outside its long beak. I am suddenly so angry. Red rage washes over my body. "You're not here, you're what my brain created to deal with it all."

Her voice stays kind and calm in her projected stillness. "That's right honey. I know that was hard for you. We need to make sure you don't slip up around Daniel or the lawyers, right? It's time for you to do this on your own." Tears form in my eyes as reality meets my fantasy. I never reconnected with Brigit. I recreated her as I had with dead little Patrick to deal with the pain and grief of my life.

I sniff, trying to stifle the emotion now invading every part of my face. I am about to lose my best friend again. The blonde statue is already fading in my sight. "Don't cry Birdie." She says lightly. "We worked so hard on your makeup and you don't want a puffy face today." I nod solemnly. The red rage makes another wave, followed by a chill of loneliness.

I put out my cigarette. She's right, well, I'm right. I don't want to cry off all my makeup. Ken Brennan, my attorney - not Bri's - will be here in ten minutes or so. He's been wonderful through all this. Understanding and compassionate and utterly ruthless in his sneak attack on Daniel. Initially, I had no desire to make this contentious. I just wanted to be free. However, once I saw our financial papers, the real ones, where Daniel had squirreled away most of the blood money from our son's death settlement and not donated it as promised - I was livid. And when his private investigator showed me pictures of my husband, undressed, embracing two different blondes - I wanted blood.

Of course, there was the first blond I caught him with. I look back to where I'd just imagined her form. My best friend in the world. My greatest comfort in my horrible loss was stolen by his inability to keep it in his pants. My visit with Dad helped me remember the details, catching them in his SUV like teenagers.

I looked around the gorgeous loft, proud of what I've built. My broken brain had to take a weird path to get here, but I'm thrilled none-the-less. DJ loves it too and will happily spend 60% of his time here, if all goes as planned today. He took the news rather well, expressing I was a better mom now and independence will be great for me. An alarm on my phone tells me it's time to meet Ken downstairs. I check my blue blazer and chic blue pants in the giant mirror one last time and ready myself for the end. And the beginning.

***

I walk toward the grocery store and see a young woman with an overly full cart headed to her minivan. She admires my cute, electric toy of a car - shiny black and still sticker new. I remember being wistful of little, sporty cars. Minivans aren't for me anymore.

I see lots of boxed frozen foods in her cart, chicken nuggets, corn dogs, and tater tots. She must have small kids. I don't envy her. Those days weren't always the funnest. I imagine her four kids are loud, fun balls of hyper energy, all under five. They also have a saintly golden retriever named Max. She's hoping to return to work someday but not until the youngest is in full time school. Her weekly trip to the grocery store is the only peace she gets; her mother-in-law watches the kids. Her husband works extra shifts when he can but is really present, involved dad. They met in college and they shared a dream of a huge family.

You can't find the fridge handle under all the beloved finger paintings and all four kids live for Elmo and swing sets. Their house is always a mess but filled with endless love and laughter. I smile for their good fortune and happiness.

I elect for the small, black cart. I'm just getting some cheese and bread and a bottle of wine. I've got glass blowing class tonight and will have a picnic with myself on the rooftop terrace after.

Made in the USA
Middletown, DE
28 July 2022

70092665R00149